falling for her enemy

a Still Harbor book

VICTORIA JAMES

Entangled Publishing, LLC
2614 South Timberline Road
Suite 109
Fort Collins, CO 80525
Visit our website at www.entangledpublishing.com.

Bliss is an imprint of Entangled Publishing, LLC. For more information on our titles, visit http://www.entangledpublishing.com/category/bliss

Edited by Alethea Spiridon Hopson
Cover design by Heather Howland
Cover art from iStock

Manufactured in the United States of America

First Edition November 2015

Bliss

Dear Reader, I absolutely love writing romances set in small towns that are filled with huge personalities. Add in the bonus of the holiday season and I'm over-the-top happy. There's nothing like imagining a town filled with people and places that evoke a sense of community and family. I imagine Still Harbor to be a town with a little bit of mystery, a lot of charm, and some of the nicest people you'll ever meet.

I'm so thrilled that this November, I will have two holiday romances to share with you. To make things even more fun, the hero in this book, Hayden Brooks also makes an appearance in my other holiday release, *The Billionaire's Christmas Proposal*. The two are long-time friends and both end up in situations they could have never imagined...but they'll end up finding their happily-ever-afters with women who challenge and love them.

Thank you so much for taking the ride into Still Harbor with me.

Happy Holidays

Victoria James

xoxo

Prologue

Hayden Brooks gazed blankly at the woman who was apparently supposed to mean something to him.

He stared and stared, trying to figure out why she was supposed to be significant to him. There was a vague familiarity about her, sort of like remembering a fading dream hours after waking. She was tall, sleek, with jet-black hair that hung straight down past her shoulders. She was attractive in an unapproachable sort of way. Her eyes were rimmed with too much black makeup and her lips were bright red, a contrast to her flawless porcelain skin. Why didn't he remember her name? And why was she standing on his doorstep?

"You don't know who I am, do you? You *are* Hayden Brooks, right?"

He gave a short nod and leaned against the doorjamb trying to look casual even though every single muscle in his body was now tightly wound. He wanted to appear casual.

He wanted her to feel at ease and let her guard down so he could figure out what was going on.

"We hooked up about seven years ago."

"Seven *years* ago?" He could barely remember the names of the women he'd dated last year. Not that there had been that many. They just hadn't been that memorable.

She nodded, her bright red lips thinning. She obviously didn't like being forgettable. "Yes, it was at The Oceanside Bar. You were there with a bunch of guys and I was there with my girlfriends... We hooked up and spent a great night together at the Oceanside Hotel."

He ran his hand over his jaw, his eyes not leaving hers. He remembered, vaguely. It had been a bad night for him, a bad week. She had been available and pursued him.

"So what are you doing here now?"

She pulled a newspaper out of her large black purse and handed it to him. He stared at the picture of himself. He'd been on the cover of the city's newspaper last week. He had just closed the biggest real estate deal in the city's history. The article was flattering. It spotlighted the father-son success team that made up Brooks Building Group. "I only knew your first name that night... We didn't really exchange information after. I had no way of contacting you again. Then last week I was drinking my morning coffee and saw your face on the cover of the newspaper. It's not really a face a girl forgets."

He didn't say anything.

"I tried looking everywhere for you seven years ago. I went back to the Oceanside, but you were never there. I asked at the hotel, they didn't know."

"Why were you looking for me?"

"Because I was pregnant."

Hell no. Hayden looked past her, into the distance, listening as the rain pounded the ground, trying to focus on a sight that would calm him down. It was a typical Vancouver fall morning—typical except for the fact that there was a woman claiming to have been pregnant by him. *Seven years ago.* He looked at her again, searching her blue eyes for something. It was impossible, really. He was the most cautious man on the planet. There was no way he'd ever risk getting someone pregnant. He had made mistakes as a teen. He'd learned to look at himself in the mirror again, but it had taken a long time, and he'd learned responsibility the hard way. He was also a man that didn't make the same mistake twice.

"No, there's no way I got you pregnant."

She gave a small smirk, unbuttoned her trench coat, revealing a lithe figure in a skin-tight black dress. "Now, I know you must be thinking that there's no way this body could have ever had a baby, but it's true."

"That wasn't what I was thinking at all. Here's what I'm thinking." He pushed himself off the doorjamb and stood straight up. No one tried to screw with him, and not about something like this. This was life altering. This would mess with his carefully controlled life. It would bring out demons he'd long since buried. "I'm thinking you saw that article, remembered our night together, and thought you could cash in."

She blinked furiously, but not before he saw her eyes fill with tears. He wasn't backing down. "I would never do that. I'm doing my civic duty and letting you know that you're a father."

"Well, then where's my kid?"

She lifted her chin. "I don't know."

Alarm bells were going off, and a slow sweat was now trucking down his spine. "How do you not know where your child is?"

"I gave her up for adoption right after birth."

He shut his eyes for a second and searched for remnants of a prayer from his childhood. He came up blank. This wasn't happening.

"I understand that if word got out you impregnated some woman, took off, and denied that you had a child, and refused to provide for said child, it would be damaging to a person of your stature."

His eyes snapped open, his gaze locked on hers. There it was. The blackmail, the motive.

"So I'm here to help you out. You give me one million, and I'll keep my mouth shut."

Blood roared in his ears and it took him a full ten seconds to find the words. He leaned forward. "I'm not paying you a dime. You're an opportunistic liar."

She held her hand to his mouth. "Opportunistic, yes. Liar? Not so much. I had a baby girl. You had a baby girl, though by now I'd say she's six. But don't worry. She's been adopted. You don't have to do anything. Pay me, I'll keep my mouth shut, and we can both go on with our separate lives."

He grabbed hold of her wrist and firmly moved it away from his mouth. "I'm not paying you a freaking dime."

She shrugged. "That's fine. Your loss."

"If I have a kid out there, I'm going to find her."

She frowned. "Wow, I didn't expect that."

"Where is she?"

She shrugged. "No idea. Handed over my rights. I don't even know her name. You can go ahead and *try* to find her."

Shame and fear washed over him with the force of unrelenting waves. He cleared his throat, trying to focus, for now, until he was in private.

"But no matter what, you need to pay out."

"I'm paying you nothing."

"Then prepare to have your name dragged through the mud."

There were very few moments in his life when he was at a loss for words. He'd always had a sharp tongue and wit in business dealings. This had rendered him speechless, because it wasn't business, it was personal and she was unknowingly bringing out all of his old demons. He didn't give a crap about his name, but his father did. His father was eighty years old, and he and Hayden had been through many rough years together. He couldn't do that to him. He needed time to fix this. He ran his hands through his hair.

"Give me a few months."

She crossed her arms and smirked. "No."

"Fine. Until Christmas. That's the best offer you'll get from me, so I suggest you take it."

"Then what?"

"We'll see. But if she's not mine, you'll regret ever coming to my door and trying to blackmail me." There was no way in hell he was planning on paying a woman that had abandoned a child that might be his and not come forward for years. He held her gaze and saw the exact moment doubt trickled into her expression.

He had it all. He had extreme wealth, homes in his favorite parts of the world, a fleet of cars, and every luxury he could ever want. He loved his job. He loved running his company. He loved acquiring business and real estate and turning them into something spectacular. But if he had a daughter out there, none of it mattered. Every success he'd ever achieved would mean nothing if he'd had a daughter that was living in foster care. All of it brought him back to the worst day of his life.

He looked at the woman staring at him. If she was telling the truth, if he had a daughter out there, nothing was going to stop him from finding her. He would find his little girl and try and make all of this right.

He'd find her and bring her back home with him.

Chapter One

If the Grinch himself had walked into the bakery, eaten all the pastries, stolen all the candy canes from the tree in the window, and the cash out of the till, it would still have been a more promising Christmas than the impending one. It was like every day brought more bad news.

Alexandra McAllister stared through blurry, tired eyes at Mrs. Cooper who was currently wringing her wrinkled hands and frowning.

"I'm so, *so* sorry my dear. I know you had your heart set on buying this bakery from me in five years, but I can't wait that long." The elderly woman grabbed one of the old-fashioned candy canes in the glass jar beside the cash register, ripped off the plastic wrapping, and broke off a piece with her false teeth. Alex watched her, wondering if the hard candy might pull Mrs. Cooper's dentures loose. She tried to be a good friend to the woman she had grown to adore, even though this news was disastrous. She was able to keep this in perspective. She could do that. She was calm and collected.

Or maybe she was reacting so calmly because nothing compared to the news her soon-to-be brother-in-law Matt Lane had delivered last month. Matt was a private investigator and had shaken her world when he'd sat her down and told her that his new client thought he might be Cassy's father. At first she'd clung to the hope that maybe this was all a mistake, but the evidence pointed to the fact that this man, Hayden Brooks, could be Cassy's biological father. They still needed to do a paternity test—nothing was certain until that happened.

"You shouldn't be worried about me with everything you have going on. I understand. This wasn't meant to be. You have to take care of you and your husband." At least she had come up with something polite to say. It was true. She was just leaving out the part about how this would completely screw up her plans and would mess with her need to provide security for her daughter.

Mrs. Cooper's eyes filled with tears again, and she waved the candy cane around. "Oh my dear, if only I could give you the bakery. But now that Martin had that awful stroke and I have to find a retirement home for us to live in, I won't have the money. I need every penny, because those places are a fortune."

"I know, of course. There will be other bakeries. I'll have more opportunities come my way," she said, lying. She grabbed a candy cane and began eating with her soon to be former employer. They crunched in silence a few minutes, both of them too agitated to lick and enjoy. She knew she had so much to be grateful for—a home, a fresh start in Still Harbor, her family, and most of all her adopted daughter,

Cassandra. But owning her own bakery would have been the security she needed for the future. In five years she would have been able to do it. She would have squirreled away money each year. Mrs. Cooper had already given her the figure she needed in order to buy. Except poor Mr. Cooper had suffered a stroke, and they were left with no choice but to sell now. There was no way she could come up with the money on such short notice.

"What about a small business loan, dear? I know that would be taking on more of a burden, but we know this bakery makes excellent money. Surely Mr. Tuttle over at the bank would help you with a payment plan. Maybe I could put in a good word."

"I wouldn't be approved. I've taken on a mortgage with my sisters for the house, and I have Cassandra's expenses. It would be too much. I know I wouldn't get the loan."

"Oh dear, oh dear," the elderly woman said. "And right before Christmas too."

Alex swallowed the last bit of her candy cane and decided she needed to ditch the self-pity long enough for Mrs. Cooper to feel better and leave. Then she would wallow in pity privately in the form of an assortment of Christmas cupcakes. "Well, it's closing time now anyway. You should get home. It's been a long day. Don't worry about me. I'll figure something out," she said, forcing a smile on her face. Right. Figure something out.

She gave another fake smile as Mrs. Cooper made her way to the front of the store. "I'll be sure to lock up and put up the closed sign," Mrs. Cooper called out.

Alex barely heard her. She was busy sinking behind the old cash desk. On her way down she managed to grab the box of cupcakes she had planned on bringing home. She sat there, alone in the empty bakery, and wondered how the heck her life, which had finally seemed to be going so well, had just blown up this week. Ripping open the lid, she looked at the mixture of Christmas cupcakes and decided that the candy cane surprise, egg nog, and peppermint chocolate cupcakes would be her first victims.

She retrieved a takeout dish, lined up her cupcakes like three shot glasses at a bar, and prayed they'd have the same effect on her mood.

She took a bite of the first one, slowly closing her eyes and letting the sweet mix of vanilla, chocolate, and sugar take her far, far away from the place that she was in right now. Leaning her head back she tried to forget that tomorrow the life she'd carefully constructed for herself was about to be seriously jeopardized. This cupcake was going to be dedicated to misery, her current state at the moment.

She eyed the peppermint chocolate, deciding not to finish the rest of the candy cane surprise. If she ate half of each cupcake, it would be like she'd eaten only one and half, which would make her total three for the day because of her earlier samplings. She needed to start working out. More than her walk to The Sweet Spot Bakery every day— it wasn't proving enough of a counterbalance to the calories consumed. The extra fifteen pounds she had packed on was proof of that. Running could help. Her sister, Kate, and her fiancé, Matt, had invited her to join them on their jogs. Those two ran almost every morning, but they were so in shape, there was no way she'd be able to keep up. Maybe she should start training in private and then join up with them in a few months. Maybe they'd be like, "Wow, you're an amazing runner, Alex..." She stuffed the last piece of chocolate in her mouth, thinking she should make that a New Year's resolution.

"Excuse me, sorry to bother you." She almost choked on the dense cupcake in her throat when a voice, a very deep, amused voice rang out in the supposedly closed, empty bakery.

Alex swiftly wiped off the crumbs from her apron, her body humming with anxiety made even worse with the amount of sugar now running through her bloodstream.

She slowly stood, mortification drowning her, as she faced what she hoped was an early gift from Santa Claus. She tried to inconspicuously lick the crumbs from the corners of mouth as she stared into the bluest eyes and the most gorgeous face she'd ever seen. She didn't need to see a mirror to know that she was a wreck. Judging by the way the man looked like he was trying to hold back a smile, she looked even worse than a wreck. His smile was delicious, as was the slight stubble across a great jawline and the dark, inky hair that was delectably mussed up...

"Hi, sorry if I startled you. The door wasn't locked so I assumed you were still open."

Mrs. Cooper was becoming so forgetful. "No, no worries... I was just um—" She felt for the box and plate with her foot and surreptitiously tried to hide them from his line of vision. "—cleaning up for the night. Can I help you with something? We're actually closed, but I think there are still some nice baked goods to choose from."

"I'm not here for the bakery. I'm looking for Alexandra McAllister."

It was *him*. It had to be. She'd never seen this man

before, not that Still Harbor was such a tiny town that she knew everyone, but she could tell he was different. She took in the beautifully fitting black coat over a suit. The tie. The way he stood there, as though he owned the place.

This wasn't how she was supposed to meet the man who wanted to take her daughter away. She was supposed to appear strong and formidable. She was supposed to have the upper hand. Right now, she looked like an out-of-control version of the Pillsbury Doughboy's wife.

She searched his face to find similarities to Cassy's. She didn't have to look for long. Cassy had dark hair. Blue eyes as well. It was wrong of her to not be happy for her daughter and she would be if this man proved to be who he thought he was. Cassy would have a father that cared enough to track her down. She could be happy and very, very terrified at the same time, because what would bring happiness for Cassy could destroy her.

But now he was here. Who was she to deny her daughter the love of a biological father? She would have given anything to have one of her parents walk back into her life and profess their love for her, to tell her that they were here to take care of her. Who was she to take that, *him*, away from Cassy? *If* he was Cassy's father.

She looked down at her hands, which were currently braced against the worn marble counter, smudges of chocolate around a few of her nails, and squeezed her eyes shut. She wasn't ready for this. She wasn't ready to meet him, not at a disadvantage like this. She opened her eyes to find him staring at her intently, like her reaction had just told him who she was. "I'm Alexandra…Alex."

He held out his hand, face now serious. "I'm Hayden

Brooks."

She wiped the chocolate from her fingers and extended her hand. His larger one engulfed hers in a firm, no-nonsense shake.

She was not ready for him, for the problems he was bringing with him. He threatened everything she had worked for, longed for, yearned for her entire life. She had walked through hell, only to finally end up living her dream with her little girl. But now Hayden Brooks was here and determined to shatter her life.

She quickly withdrew her hand and stuffed it into the front pocket of her holly-printed apron. "You're a day early."

Hayden stared at the cute brunette who looked like she was either going to cry or reach across the counter and strangle him with his own tie. She was beautiful, undeniably, but not in a made-up, manufactured way. She wasn't decked out. In fact, she was the opposite. Her Christmas apron was covered with chocolate and was crooked, hanging loosely off her neck. Her hair was dark and shiny and at some point during the day had probably been pulled back; now most of it was hanging around her gorgeous face. Her green eyes reminded him of the color of the cedar roping he'd noticed around the bakery door, and her lips were a gorgeous, kiss-able pink except for the dark brown chocolate in the corners.

But more importantly than all that, she was the mother of his might-be daughter. What would bring a single woman to adopt a child? He'd never think of doing something like that. He'd been wondering this when he got over the shock of finding out he might have a child he never knew about. This woman had adopted Cassandra and was now raising her, and if he was Cassandra's father, he owed this woman everything.

"I thought I'd get settled into the Harbor House Inn tonight before we met tomorrow. But when I was driving through town, I saw the lights on at the bakery. I knew you worked here, so I thought I'd drop in." He was trying to keep his voice as calm and agreeable as possible. That was how he had to play this whole thing. The more this woman liked him, the easier it would be to get what he wanted, and the faster he'd be able to get out of this town and get back to work.

She stared out the window and he followed her gaze. It had been snowing on his way into town, the drive getting progressively worse as he left the city and took the rural roads to the middle of nowhere. From what he saw, it was a picturesque little town, like one of those places you'd see on a postcard. There was cedar roping on the stores in the downtown center, a big town square with a giant Christmas tree, and that overall charm that a city couldn't offer. It seemed like a great place to raise a kid, if a person didn't have any other ambitions than…family.

"Sure, not a problem. Harbor House is a nice place. It was probably a good idea to come into town tonight since we're supposed to get a bunch of snow tomorrow."

"Yeah, I'd heard about that." He didn't want to be chit-chatting but he understood he needed to be patient with her and that she was evaluating him. After speaking to his lawyer, he knew the best way to deal with all of this was by keeping it out of the court system for as long as possible. If he and the adopted mother could come to some sort of an understanding, that would be best for all of them, especially the little girl.

"So, um, Cassandra is at home right now. I live with my sisters and their kids."

He nodded. "That's great… It must be a challenge juggling everything."

Something flashed in her eyes, and she lifted her chin slightly. "Not that much of a challenge. Nothing I can't handle. It's an absolute pleasure."

He got it. "I'm here to find out if I have a daughter. We'll take things one step at a time. I think we can both agree that we only want the best for Cassandra, right?"

She nodded, her features relaxing slightly. "We'll be going to the Santa Claus parade tomorrow afternoon. Three o'clock. The whole family. If you'd like to join us, that might be a nice way to meet Cassy without her becoming suspicious of anything. Then we can take it from there."

Take it from there meant she'd scope him out some more and decide whether or not she'd let him have the paternity test taken. That was fine; he had no intention of screwing anything up. The more agreeable he was, the faster this whole thing would go and hopefully be uncomplicated. He would approach this as a real estate deal. Lure the client in, charm them, make them have faith in him and his abilities, and then close the deal. That technique had never failed him before, so why would it now?

As for kids and Santa Claus parades…he'd have to fake it. The last kid he'd spent any time with was on the flight from Vancouver to Toronto, and it hadn't been pleasant. The whining had set his nerves on edge, but luckily earphones had drowned that out; he didn't expect he'd be able to do that with his own kid. He cleared his throat, realizing that Alex was staring at him, looking worried. "So where should I meet you?"

"We can meet right outside the bakery. It's a good spot, and if the kids get cold, they can come in here and warm up."

He nodded, then nudged his chin in the direction of her phone that was sitting on the counter. "Do you have any pictures of her? Can I see one?"

Her mouth dropped open slightly, but she nodded after a few seconds and picked up her phone. Her wallpaper was a picture of her and Cassandra. Her hand trembled as she passed him the phone. Emotion, the kind that snuck up on a guy, ambushed him until all his senses were awake. He studied the little girl who was beaming at the camera. She had the kind of smile that could make a stranger smile. Alexandra was holding her, and they were on a swing. They looked…happy, like one of those stock photography pictures of a mother and daughter in a new picture frame.

He cleared his throat. "She's really cute."

"I think so."

He continued to search the picture. She had dark hair and blue eyes, but that didn't mean anything…much… except that it was the same as his…and his mother's.

"I guess you're probably looking for a resemblance?"

He looked up. She was staring back at him, insecurity stamped on every lovely feature. This entire thing was kind of surreal—finding out he may have a daughter, tracking her down to this small town, and then meeting the woman who had adopted her. He felt warm, and he didn't know if it was the bakery filled with the comforting smells of cinnamon and sugar, the large Christmas tree in the great big store window with its faded multi-colored lights, or the melancholic sound of Nat King Cole's voice softly singing in the background. Snow was falling outside, blanketing the already pretty town in a sheet of white, making him believe for a second in fate and destiny. Was this all supposed to happen like this? Was this the way his life was supposed to play out? Maybe it was a second chance for him, a chance to correct the biggest regret of his life.

Shit, he'd better get it together before he turned into Norman Rockwell. He rolled his shoulders and passed her phone back. Less than an hour in this town and he was turning into a sap. Get it together, man. He needed to get back to his room at the inn, go over the proposal for work, and then review his strategy for this…situation.

"Maybe she looks more like her mother?" Her eyes darted away from him. "Or maybe that was silly for me to say. I mean you probably don't even know what her mother looked like if you guys met in a bar and it was dark and you had a one-night stand. Who knows if you could even rec… I think I'm going to stop talking now," she said, her face matching the red trim on her apron.

He coughed. Obviously she was aware of the details because of her close relationship with Matt. He'd had to be as candid as possible with Matt during their meeting; divulging details with a stranger hadn't been pleasant. "It's fine. I, uh, will meet you all here tomorrow then," he said, backing up a step.

"Oh, wait. Remember, I'm just saying you're a friend. That's it. Then you and I can talk about this after…without Cassy around."

Her anxiety was palpable, transforming her face, aging her in a way that should have made him feel guilty. "Okay."

He walked out, the sound of the jingling bells on the door trailing behind him as he stepped onto the sidewalk, the cold, heavy air greeting him.

He knew enough now. He knew that the feeling of responsibility, of connection, of what was his, had kicked in. He knew enough about himself that when the emotion had coursed through his body, seeing that little girl in the picture, that if she was his, he wasn't walking away from this. He would approach this like he approached everything else in his life—with stealthy determination, his mind securely focused on the end goal. No matter how grateful he was to Cassy's adoptive mother, he would not walk away from his little girl.

Chapter Two

"I'm sorry, guys, it's going to be a late dinner," Alex called out from the entryway, dropping her bag to the floor and shutting the door. She had talked to herself the whole way home, reassuring pep talks. Nothing had happened. Hayden Brooks couldn't take away her little girl. Yet.

Cassy raced toward her and gave her a hug that threw her backward and onto the front rug with a thud. Normally she would have laughed. Tonight she just held onto her little girl even tighter.

"Ah! You're killing me, Mommy!" Cassy laughed, struggling to get free.

Alex gave her a kiss and stood, hanging up her jacket. "How was school?"

"Great! Except at recess there was an alliteration," she said, hands on her hips, a deep frown on her cute face. Her daughter had a passion for using long words, except she always used them in the wrong context.

She hung up her coat and stifled her smile. "Are you sure you mean *alliteration*?"

Cassy was nodding at her and about to defend her word choice when Alex's sister, Cara Hamilton, walked into the room. "Don't worry about dinner. Matt and Kate are bringing it home."

"Hi, Auntie Alex," Beth, Cara's daughter said as she walked into the hallway.

"Hi, sweetie."

The door opened, and Matt, Kate, and Janie came in. The three girls immediately ambushed Matt with squeals of "Uncle Matt!" He hugged all of them, handing the bags of takeout to Kate and took turns indulging them in spins and pretend drops to the ground.

Matt brought a completely different dynamic to their family. He doted on all three girls, and they adored him. Up until that point, she hadn't given the absence of a male figure in their lives much thought. But the way they reacted to him made it obvious that maybe something was missing from their lives. And Kate had changed so much. Kate had been the most…anal of the three of them, but now she had a more relaxed look about her. Alex didn't know if it was because she was sleeping with a hot man every night or if it was that she finally truly trusted a man. They were in love. The kind of love Alex always hoped was possible but hadn't come remotely close to experiencing.

"I'm going to set the table. Thanks for getting dinner," Alex said once they'd all exchanged greetings. She knew her sisters would follow her—they'd been very watchful ever since the news of Hayden.

Sure enough, as she was setting out the plates, Kate

walked in and got right into it. "I want you to know that this is all going to be okay. We'll be right there tomorrow when you meet him."

She set the last plate down and looked over at Kate. "I already met him."

Cara gasped; she was standing in the doorway. "Omigod, when were you going to tell us?"

"I just walked in. He appeared out of nowhere...while I was stuffing cupcakes down my throat due to another unexpected catastrophe." She was still infuriated at the way she'd met Hayden. She had wanted to be seen as a formidable opponent, not a flake. She marched over to grab the cutlery. Kate moved out of her way.

"Okay, which catastrophe are we tackling first?" Cara asked, walking into the room and grabbing drinks from the fridge.

"Neither. I don't want to deal with any of it. I want to drown my sorrows in a bottle of any red wine we have in the house."

"Okay, done. It's only three hours until the girls' bedtime. But first you have to tell us about him," Kate said. Alex watched her fill up the dinner glasses with ease. They had a whole routine. They were all comfortable in their lives together. Yes, things were changing because of Matt, but it was all positive change, wanted change. This Hayden guy threatened everything. The life she deserved was going to be taken away.

"What's he like?" Cara asked. She saw the worried look that passed between her and Kate.

Alex set the forks down, resisting the urge to jab one into the wood of the table. "He's...I don't know. He seems like a perfectly normal, perfectly nice man." She wasn't going to say a word about the fact that Cassy's might-be-father was unbelievably good-looking, because that was useless. Pointless. It was ironic, really. The only conversation she'd had with a hot guy was about him ruining her life.

"Oh," Cara mumbled, coming forward and standing beside Kate. "What did he say?"

"Did it go well?" asked Kate.

"You mean besides the fact that he witnessed me stuffing three cupcakes in my mouth? And that I had cupcake batter all over my fingernails and probably crumbs on my face? You mean besides that? Or the fact that he was probably judging me and wondering what kind of sugar-beast had adopted his child? Or maybe, just maybe, you are referring to the fact that Mrs. Cooper needs to sell her business now and can't wait five years for me to buy it. Maybe you're referring to that."

"I think I'm going to get wine now," Kate whispered, giving her a quick hug before she went to the wine rack in the dining room.

"Omigod, Alex," Cara whispered, pulling out a chair and sitting.

Kate was back and handed her a glass of wine. "Okay, one thing at a time. The bakery isn't lost. We'll come up with a way to help you, and this guy, well, we don't know if he's even her father," she said, lowering her voice.

She spoke into her wine glass, voicing the thought that had plagued her since meeting Hayden. "No, but I had a feeling…like, I don't know…"

"I think you're scared, and you're already anticipating this is going to go badly. Matt said he seems like a good guy.

You know he ran that background check for you before starting this."

"The one that said he's loaded? The one that basically confirmed that he could afford to tie this up in court until he wins full custody over Cassy, and that I may never—"

"Nope, not happening. You've got to stop thinking like that."

She glanced through the doorway that led to the family room where Matt and the girls were playing. "What if he takes her away from me?" she whispered, watching Cassy sneak up behind Matt and poke him in the back, trying to scare him. It was her greatest fear, losing Cassy. The idea of not having her in her life was devastating. Children weren't supposed to leave. Children needed their parents. This should have been guaranteed. This should have been safe. Cassy was supposed to be her little girl forever. And what if he took her away and Cassy thought she'd abandoned her?

"Let me rephrase it—not going to happen."

She stared at Kate and Cara, knowing they'd never get it, the desperate way she needed Cassy. Yes, they'd all been through their own hell growing up. Yes, they'd all been strong, survivors, but they each had their own unique memories, and those memories had impacted each of them differently. She knew her memories, her issues, were only making this situation more terrifying. "If he's her father, who am I to prevent her from being with him?"

"You're her mother, the only mother she's ever known. The first person to ever truly want her. You adopted her. You gave her a home, love, and everything a child needs," Cara whispered, standing beside them.

Alex covered her face with her hands, and she felt Kate's

and Cara's arms around her. She had no idea what she'd do without any of them. She knew that all of them were connected, despite their lack of true familial ties. "You need to be strong. You can't break down now. And besides, if Cassy sees you crying, she's going to come in here and demand answers."

Alex nodded, taking a deep breath and trying to shake it off. "I just… It sounds childish, but it's not fair. We're supposed to be busy with Christmas plans and the girls. I never once thought I'd be standing here scared out of my mind that I was going to lose my little girl."

"It's too soon to freak out. Remember, if you decide to let Hayden do the paternity test and he's not her father, he will walk out of your life and this will be a distant nightmare. You'll be making Christmas dinner and the girls will be opening presents from Santa, and it will be the best Christmas," Kate said.

Alex blinked away tears. "I don't ever want her to think that I left her, that I abandoned her."

"Okay, you have to stop," Cara said. "Drink that," she said, pointing to the wine.

Alex took a sip. "Great. By the time this is done I'm going to be an alcoholic and sugar addict."

Kate clinked her glass against hers. "We won't let that happen."

"And what's this about Mrs. Cooper?"

Alex took a longer sip of wine. "I can't deal with that right now too. Let's save that for after the girls' bedtime."

"Done," Cara said. "So what's the plan for tomorrow?"

Alex took a deep breath and then another sip of wine. "He's meeting us at the parade. I'm introducing him as a friend. We'll all watch him and analyze him for signs of crazy... Then we take it from there."

Kate nodded. "Perfect. We can handle that. In a couple of weeks, this will all be over, Cassy will still be yours, and we'll have the best Christmas ever, okay?"

Right. Hayden Brooks might not be Cassy's father. This could all be one big mistake and then he would disappear from their lives forever.

Hayden looked out the bay window of his suite at The Harbor House Inn, taking a sip of his coffee. He had set up his makeshift office on the antique desk in front of the window; papers were already covering it, his laptop in the middle. It would do. He'd stayed up late trying to catch up on everything he'd missed yesterday at the office. It was probably the worst time to leave work, with the hotel deal they'd been trying to land. Just last month they'd made headlines for the single largest real estate deal in the city, but of course neither he nor his father were satisfied with that. They were about to beat their own record just a month later if they managed to get the contract to build the exclusive oceanfront hotel. Nothing had ever come close to beating the thrill of acquisition.

He finished his coffee and shut his laptop, looking around the room. The Inn was quaint, his room the best one in the small building. His assistant always booked the best; it was how he'd grown up. In Still Harbor, though, the best was adequate, not luxurious. Charming. He didn't mind. He thought the character in the historical inn had a coziness to it that was missing from his everyday life. The room had a king-size four-poster bed that was an antique reproduction. There was a fireplace that looked original to the building, and everything had been clean and cozy. It was the type of room a woman would probably appreciate more than he, but he didn't know the type of women who appreciated cozy.

An image of Alexandra popped into his head. She would appreciate this kind of room. She didn't seem stuck-up, and there was a warmth about her that he'd detected right away, along with the other things he'd noticed right away—the stunning features and the wariness in her eyes. Beyond that, he didn't know because of the frumpy Christmas apron she'd been wearing. He rolled his shoulders wondering why the hell he was even thinking about her. He chalked it up to habit. Well, he'd rein that in. He never let personal feelings get in the way of a business transaction, so there was no way he'd let it now.

He had a few minutes before it was time to meet up with Alexandra and Cassy. The weight in his chest that had accompanied him from the moment he found out he potentially had a kid was still there. Maybe worse now. He was going to meet her today; he was going to meet her family. He was going to be judged by her adoptive mother to see if he "met" her standards. This was a departure for him, taking a step back and letting someone else take the lead. He knew it was the smart play for now. There was no point in getting Alexandra's defenses up. And he did owe her for taking his child in. He would always be grateful for that, but he wouldn't let her get away with not allowing him a paternity test. If it proved to be positive, then there was no way he'd hop on a plane halfway across the country and only see his daughter a few times a year.

His phone rang, and after a few seconds, he found it under a stack of files. It was his father requesting FaceTime. He groaned. There were some things his father didn't have a stellar grasp of, and FaceTiming was one of them.

"Hi, Dad, how are you?"

He was greeted by a close up of his father's nostril.

"Good, good, son."

"Dad, can you please hold your phone away from your face a little?"

After some muttering, Hayden was finally looking at his father's face—on a diagonal but whatever.

"Just calling to check in on you and see if you met the little girl yet."

The image of Cassy on Alexandra's phone popped into his mind, and he smiled faintly. "No, but I saw a picture of her."

His father lurched forward, and he was staring at the nostril again. "And? Any resemblance?"

Hayden didn't want to say it aloud, but knew his father was desperate for hope. He didn't bother correcting him this time because he didn't want to see the expression on his face. "She looks like me…like Mom."

There was a long pause on the other end of the phone. "Did you meet the adoptive mother?"

"Yes, I met Alexandra."

"What's she like?"

Cute, sweet…defensive. "She has her guard up. That's only natural though. I can't blame her for that. Seems like a nice enough person."

"Well, know that whatever happens, I've got your back.

If you need anything, I can be on the next flight to Toronto. Hayden, if she's yours, you bring that little girl home where she belongs. She can go to your old schools. We'll give her the best of everything. If she's a Brooks, then we need to treat her like one."

Hayden attempted a smile. His father was eighty, and though he was in good shape, he was showing signs of his age. There was no way Hayden would ask him to jump on a plane for emotional support. He wasn't even sure what that meant. And he was pretty damn sure his father had even less of an idea. He and his father were close, but they weren't exactly the affectionate type. His mother had filled that role in their lives. She had been all about emotion; she was warm and funny, and so loving. She had doted on them and had been the love of his father's life. Hayden knew that his father had never really gotten over losing her. Even though she had died so many years ago, neither of them had gotten over her loss. Cassy would mean the world to his father... to him.

"Thanks, Dad, I'll keep you posted. Take care of yourself."

"You too, Hayden."

He ended the call and walked across the room, grabbing his coat and gloves. He had no idea what to expect. Parades weren't exactly his form of entertainment, and he hadn't been to a parade of any kind since he was a kid, with his parents.

He made his way down to the lobby, forcing a smile on his face as staff at the front desk smiled and waved. Small towns definitely had the whole hospitality thing down. He walked by the enormous tree in the lobby, pausing as he observed a father holding a small child, letting him touch the twinkling lights. This was the first time he'd even noticed something like this. He'd never paid much attention to kids or families when he was out.

He shrugged off the foreign feeling and walked outside. He stood on the sidewalk and buttoned up his coat, the temperature reminding him how much colder this part of the country was. He was used to the mild winters of Vancouver. Small clusters of people were already forming on the sidewalks, and he made his way toward the Sweet Spot Bakery. He passed the groups of people, the chatter and excited laughter of children thundering in his ears as he walked. They were loud. Little people were very, very loud.

The Sweet Spot Bakery came into view. His heart thumped as his gaze wandered over the people standing in front of it. This would be the first glimpse of his daughter. He recognized Matt Lane. He had flown out to meet him last month and had hired him instantly. Since then they'd corresponded almost daily. He was the only guy with three very good-looking women and three little girls. He studied each girl, looking for the one he'd memorized in the picture on Alex's iPhone.

The first little girl had glasses and appeared to have Down's syndrome. The second little girl had blonde hair. The third little girl…a lump formed in his throat and he stuffed his hands in his pockets. She could be his. She was currently tugging on Matt's arm. Alexandra leaned down and said something in her ear. She crossed her arms and from where he was standing, he could make out a disgruntled expression. Hell. That could be his kid. He should be there. He should be the guy whose arm she was tugging on. He should be picking her up or doing whatever it is dads did with their kids.

Hayden walked forward, increasing his pace as a need inside him took over his rational thought. His gaze connected with Alexandra's, and that lump increased as he read the fear across her features.

"Good morning," he said, hoping his voice sounded normal. The girls peered up at him. The three women were giving him looks he didn't really feel like analyzing at the moment.

"Hey, nice to see you again, Hayden," Matt said, giving him a slap on the back. He liked him, and he was relieved to see him. His reputation was stellar. When Matt had uncovered that Cassy could be his daughter, he had tread both sides very cautiously. Matt had been aboveboard with everything, including telling him that he was going to do a background check on him. And then telling him, off the record, that if he was some kind of asshole, he'd make him regret it. He had to respect a guy like that. He protected the people he loved. Hayden knew he'd have done the same in his situation.

"Hi," Alex said and gave him a forced smile. He was introduced to the rest of them, but his eyes lingered on Cassy. She gave him a bright smile that made his heart stop for a second because it was so damn cheerful and trusting. She was missing her front teeth, but that didn't seem to bother her. She was wearing a hat that had some funny-looking cat on it that he felt like he should recognize, along with a bright pink snowsuit. All the kids were in snowsuits.

"Do you like parades?" He didn't know what to say to a kid, especially a kid that might be his, but it felt like an appropriate question.

Cassy must have agreed because she beamed at him again, the missing teeth making him smile. "I love parades! And if you stand close enough to the road, you might even catch some candy when they throw it."

He didn't have to worry about conversation because the girls took over chattering about things as the parade started.

"How are you doing?" he asked, bending slightly to speak closer to Alexandra's ear. He caught the faint scent of vanilla.

She turned to look up at him. "I guess as good as I could be, considering." Her cheeks were rosy from the cold, and he found himself distracted by her mouth. Her lips were full, plump even, with a shiny gloss over them, reminding him of Christmas red. Her lips matched the hat she was wearing, and her dark hair framed her face and hung loosely over her red jacket. She was…beautiful, not that it mattered, but he'd always had a weakness for beautiful things.

"So, Mr. Hayden, what's your favorite part of the parade?"

He glanced down in the direction of the little voice. His… well, Cassy was staring up at him. Her voice was sweet, with a lot of spunk. He liked that. He liked thinking his daughter might be a bit of a ball-breaker. What was his favorite part of a parade… He felt Alexandra's gaze on him, and he knew Cassy was staring at him expectantly. "I haven't been to a parade in a really, really long time."

"You don't look that old."

He laughed. "Thanks. I guess when Mr. and Mrs. Claus make their appearance."

Cassy nodded wisely. His answer had been acceptable. He stood with them, as though he belonged there, as though he was a friend of the family. He felt an unexpected jolt of guilt. The reality of what he was doing here would actually destroy their family. He jammed his hands into his coat pocket and pretended to give a crap about the grouping of Grinches that were now walking down the boulevard in a row. But all he could think of was that the little girl in the front row who was madly waving at the Grinch and his ridiculous dog prancing down the street could be his daughter.

He glanced over at the woman beside him who was currently sneezing. The pom-pom on her red hat bobbed back and forth with the movement. "Cold?"

She shook her head. "No, I'm fine." She looked up at him, and then away, but not before he caught the flash of irritation.

"How long does this go on for?"

"Should be over soon. Then we're all getting hot chocolate."

He nodded, noticing the reluctance in her voice. "We need to speak in private."

She looked straight ahead, her refined features barely moving. "Maybe tonight, after I put Cassy to bed. I don't want this day to be ruined for her."

"I have no intention of ruining her day," he whispered, cringing at the harshness in his voice.

She stiffened, tilting her chin up. "Of course."

"It's Santa!" the girls screamed. All the kids started jumping up and down, and he stood there, taking it all in, the approaching float, the kids, and his potential daughter. The entire situation was absurd. He was standing in a picture-perfect small town, Christmas spirit everywhere, acting like he belonged here. If it weren't for the gorgeous woman beside him, making it very clear in her body language and tone that he definitely didn't belong here, he'd almost believe it.

Once the appearance of Mr. and Mrs. Claus was over, they made their way into the bakery. A blast of warmth and the smell of cinnamon and coffee greeted them.

"All right, my treat," Matt said, as the kids scrambled to a large table by the front window. There was a flurry of activity, scarves and hats and jackets being pulled off. He followed Matt to the front cash register, remembering last night when he'd first met Alex. He didn't want to acknowledge the immediate attraction to her; doing so would be pointless. Also, it wouldn't exactly help him with his goal.

"What are you having?" Matt asked peering through the glass case.

"Just a coffee."

Matt straightened up, ordered a dozen cookies shaped like Christmas trees, three hot chocolates, and five coffees. While the young woman busied herself with the order, he turned to him. Matt was the kind of guy you'd want as a friend, not an enemy. "How are things going?"

He shrugged. "Not really going anywhere at the moment. I'm going to speak with Alex tonight."

Matt nodded, handing over a few bills to the cashier, and waved off his attempt to pay. "Alex is like a sister to me," he said, his voice hard as he leaned against the counter and eyed him as though he was contemplating kicking his ass.

Hayden stood a little straighter and stared right back. "I think you already gave me this lecture."

Matt pushed off the counter to stand eye-to-eye with him. "Well, I'm giving you a refresher."

Hayden reigned in his temper along with his rebuttal. "It's been noted."

Matt accepted the box of cookies while giving him a tough look. "Don't mess with her."

"I'm here to find out if Cassandra is my kid. That's all. I'm not here to screw with anyone's life."

Matt gave him a terse nod, then slapped him on the back. "Good, just wanted to make sure."

Hayden grabbed the two cardboard trays of beverages, and they walked back to the table. He sat down beside Alex, noticing the way she stiffened. Matt passed around the cookies, and he handed out the coffees. Minutes later the conversation was lively, the bakery packed as parade goers streamed through. Christmas carols blasted and it was chaos. He just wanted to have a private conversation with Alex and get her to agree to a paternity test.

"So, Cassy what grade are you in?"

She looked up from trying to fish marshmallows out of her drink. "Grade one."

"How do you like it?"

She grinned triumphantly when she grabbed a marsh-mallow, not minding one bit that hot chocolate was now dribbling down her arm. Alex leaned forward and wiped it up with a napkin. "It's okay, but even if it wasn't, there's not much I could do about it since there's only one school in Still Harbor anyway."

"One school?" He frowned and turned to Alex. "Isn't there a private school around here? At least within busing proximity?"

He glanced over at Matt when he heard a choking sound. He should have taken that as a warning, especially when

Matt then leaned back in his chair and stretched out his legs and looked at him as though he was about to watch the game on TV. Hayden slowly turned to face the other women at the table when he noticed how quiet everyone was. Was it the private school comment? All three women looked like they were ready to pounce on him. The girls were oblivious and currently engaged in a race to eat the most marshmallows. "There's nothing wrong with the public education system here," Cara said. She was staring at him like he had said something offensive. "I can say that with authority since I'm an elementary school teacher on the board."

He stifled his groan by taking a sip of coffee. No wonder Matt was grinning. He'd walked into a trap. "Just wondering. I know rural areas don't have the best reputation."

Kate leaned forward and glared at him. "Still Harbor has an excellent elementary and secondary education system."

"I'm sure it does, but you can't exactly compare it to private school education or when it's time to look at post-secondary."

"Cassy is in grade one," Alex said in a low voice. "I'm not concerned about her post-secondary education yet."

"It's never too early."

She leaned toward him, her green eyes sparkling with something he supposed was absolute disgust. "For you? It's too early buddy, way too early, because all this conversation may be completely irrelevant in a few weeks. So you can keep your stuck-up opinions to yourself."

"Are we still putting up the Christmas tree tomorrow?" Cassy asked, interrupting.

Alex exhaled loudly and leaned back in her chair. He caught the look between Alex and her sisters. Clearly, none of them wanted him around. Fine. He took another swig of coffee and swallowed it down. He was going to have to ease up on his education opinions for a while.

Alex snapped a Christmas tree cookie in half. "Yes, we are, but why don't you finish up what you're eating so we can go home before the snow starts?"

"And what about Blueberry Hill?" Cassy asked. She was persistent. He liked that. He also liked watching the exchange between mother and daughter. It was giving him insight into their daily life. It was also teaching him how to act around a kid.

"Cassy, I don't think we need to go over our plans right now," Alex said, handing her a napkin.

Cassy frowned, and rubbed the napkin over her mouth. The chocolate was still there. He stifled his grin. "Well, I do think we need to. I like planning upcoming holiday events."

"Why don't we worry about that when we get home?" Matt said. Hayden caught the look of relief and gratitude Alex gave him. Interesting. Matt was definitely around enough that he knew how to steer the conversation and was comfortable with the kids. Maybe his kid.

Cassy turned to him. "So, Mr. Hayden, where do you live?" She had now turned her attention to trying to fish out marshmallows with her finger and peering up at him simultaneously.

"Vancouver."

"That's in Columbia, right?"

He grinned. "British Columbia, the other end of the country."

She nodded and then dropped a marshmallow in her mouth. "Did you have to take an airplane to get here?"

He nodded. He was aware of the fact that everyone was pretending not to watch him, but they were all doing a bad job.

"I don't think I've ever been on an airplane."

Hayden didn't say anything, but he caught the look across Alex's face. Yeah, at one time Cassy must have been on an airplane, to get here.

"Neither have we," the other little girl said.

He smiled at them. "Well, it's pretty cool."

Cassy smiled back at him, a marshmallow filling the empty space between her teeth for a moment. "So you live really far away, right?"

He glanced over at Alex who kept picking up a piece of cookie and then putting it back down.

"It's pretty far, but it's still in Canada."

An elderly woman with a heavy gait came over to their table. He was thankful for the interruption. She was wringing her hands and holding a half-eaten candy cane. "Oh, Alex, thank goodness you're here! Do you think you could close up tonight? I need to get back to the nursing home because Martin isn't eating today and I'm worried sick. I wouldn't normally ask."

"No problem," Alex said as her sisters nodded. This whole shared childcare thing was interesting. Cassy looked completely okay with her mother not going home with her.

Mrs. Cooper pressed a hand to her chest and the candy cane into her mouth. "Oh, you're an angel, dear. Thank you."

Alex turned to him. "Sorry, I guess our conversation will have to wait."

He shrugged. "I'll stay." He was aware of the increased tension and all eyes on them.

She sat up a little straighter. "No need."

"Kind of. There's kind of a big need, actually."

She snapped her cookie into quarters. Her cheeks turned the color of her hat.

"Okay, well how about we all leave since it's almost time to close, that way you can get a head start," Cara said, giving Alex a pointed look.

Alex stood, ignoring him. "Sure, that's great. Good night, everyone," she said. Cassandra ran around the table to give her a big hug. "I'll try and get home before bedtime, okay," she whispered. Then he stood there and watched as she gave Cassy approximately five thousand kisses in thirty seconds. He rammed his hands into his jeans pockets as he was sidelined by a memory of his mother doing the same thing to him. He looked away, and the memory slipped from his mind, but the warmth of it lingered in a way that made him feel at peace, which was completely disconcerting. He didn't think of his mother often, mostly because whenever he did, he missed her, and then he'd be hit with the guilt over disappointing her.

Cassy nodded and they all walked out after saying their goodbyes. Bedtime. He wondered what time that was. He wondered about everything—what was a normal day like for them, where did Cassy go to school, who were her best friends…

Alex ignored him and started to clear the dishes from the table. He grabbed the paper cups and followed her to the back. Being a man accustomed to admiring all kinds of views in his line of work, he took a moment to appreciate the very fine view of the woman in front of him. She had curves in all the right places and probably the finest ass he'd seen in a long time. Unfortunately, she was the only woman in the world that was absolutely off limits to him. The swinging door would have shut on his face had he not already anticipated it and braced it open with his elbow.

"I don't need any help," she said, grabbing the cups and tossing them into a big bin. She shoved her way through the door and back out into the bakery.

"Well, I'm here anyway," he said following her. He had to admit, he kind of liked the attitude she was giving off, because it was the opposite of how she looked.

There were still customers in the bakery even though the crowd had thinned out. He leaned against the front counter, wondering how much money she could possibly make working in a place like this. Certainly didn't seem like enough to support a kid. She placed a stack of dishes back down on the counter with a sigh and a look that told him she wasn't impressed. "This isn't the time or place to discuss what we're going to do."

"Agreed, which is why I'm helping you. The sooner you finish, the sooner we can have that discussion."

She was eyeing leftover hot chocolate and he wondered if she was contemplating chucking it at him. "It will be at least an hour until the customers are all gone. Then I have another hour minimum of cleaning up and prepping for Monday."

He shrugged. "Where am I going to go? Columbia?"

That almost earned him a smile.

Chapter Three

Alex tried to ignore the 6'2" figure in The Sweet Spot bakery window, but it was proving to be a useless endeavor. The man, just by standing around doing nothing, seemed to have a presence as huge as Santa Claus. Except, of course, he looked nothing like Santa. Nope. Maybe that would have been better. A kindly, aging man who wasn't so intimidating or…virile. He was currently in front of the large picture window, hands in his jean pockets, his profile visible as he looked up at the Christmas tree. She frowned at the undeniably handsome picture he made. If he were anyone else, she'd pray he'd been sent to her as a Christmas present.

"You sure I can't help you with anything?"

She slammed the till shut. "I'm all done."

He turned to her. "Great. Let's sit and talk."

"Would you like a coffee? I have some. Food? There are a few things still left."

He shook his head. It was like he knew she was stalling.

Or contemplating spilling hot coffee on him so he'd have to go back to his hotel room and postpone their conversation. "I'm okay. Thanks."

She pulled her apron off and rounded the corner of the counter, forcing herself to look calm. Right now, she was anything but calm. Her heart was racing as though she'd just consumed a double espresso and two cupcakes. She walked over to the table he was standing beside. He motioned for her to sit down and she did.

"So how long have you lived in Still Harbor?"

She brushed at some pretend crumbs on the already wiped-down table. "A year."

"What made you come here?"

She sighed loudly. "We don't have to make chit-chat."

"I'm trying to be polite."

"No need. You're trying to be charming so that I'll like you and make things easy for you. Things are really busy right now."

"I looked into a reputable company that does paternity tests. It's quick and uncomplicated. I have the kit in my room at the inn."

Her heart beat heavily, and she frowned, looking down at the table. "Do we really need to do this over Christmas?"

He leaned forward. "I didn't fly out here and take a month off work for you to not even let me get a paternity test."

"And *I* didn't adopt a child only to have someone come in and threaten to take her away from me," she said, feeling a surge of heat move through her. His patience had obviously worn out. She tore her gaze from his and forced herself to look out the window and calm down. Snow was tumbling down at a fast rate; it had been all evening and if it were any other night, she'd be walking home, her feet kicking through freshly fallen white snow. Now the only thing she felt like kicking was the man in front of her.

"Alex, I know this isn't easy for you."

She plastered her 'I'm fine' expression on and looked up at him. His dark hair was all mussed up, and she knew from covertly staring at him all day that he had a tendency to run his hands through it. Or maybe it was because he was nervous. His blue eyes seemed darker now, and intense. He was intense. His voice was deep, but she heard the softness in it when he spoke to her, sort of like when he'd spoken to Cassy earlier. It meant he was trying to be nice, sympathetic even. She had liked that, for Cassy's sake. She should appreciate that. She should also appreciate that he seemed very normal. He had a job. Actually, he reeked of money.

He was unbelievably good-looking, not that it mattered. She wanted Cassy to have a kind father, someone who'd hold her hand and snuggle with her and be her safe haven. That's what her little girl deserved, especially if he took her away. Ugh. She was going to cry. She blinked back tears and stared at the Christmas tree. She needed to stop thinking like this.

"Alex, I get that you have a lot of questions."

She rolled her lips inward and nodded. *Way to look like a fierce opponent*. She was acting like a spineless mute. *Get it together. You're Cassy's mom, so fight.* She turned to him. "I do. The biggest one is what you plan on doing if Cassy is your daughter."

His jaw clenched, and something flashed across his eyes, but his voice was gruff with that hint of tenderness. "I want her to be happy, and I know, based on everything I saw, that she's very happy."

"You don't live here though."

"We'll figure it out. But if Cassy's mine, Vancouver is my home and I'd expect my daughter to live with me. We'd work out visitation."

Visitation, with her daughter. Cassy was *her* daughter. She'd known it the second she'd seen Cassy's picture. She had been her daughter from the moment she'd walked into her foster home. It had been Christmas, Alex's favorite time of year, and Cassy had been sleeping in a bassinet. Within minutes of her standing there, watching what had to be the most adorable baby she'd ever seen, Cassy had opened her eyes. When her blue eyes locked onto hers, Alex was gone. Cassy was everything she needed in her life and there was nothing and no one who could ever take that away. All she had ever wished for was a family—a family of her own, a child of her own. Finally she had it and now this man threatened to take it all away.

Alex sat up a little straighter and eyed Hayden squarely. "I made a promise to Cassy that I would never leave her, that I would be her mother forever and that she and I would be together forever."

He clenched his jaw and she sat there, proud her voice didn't quiver, that she sounded tough even though inside she was terrified of her little girl being taken away from her.

"Like I said, I don't want to hurt anyone, but if she's my daughter, then I plan on being a real father to her."

Alex snapped her gaze away from his and concentrated on the snow falling in soft tufts outside. Still Harbor was supposed to be the perfect place for them. This was the town all of them had wanted to belong too. Cassy loved it here. Hayden was threatening to ruin everything. She stood from the table and marched across the bakery, leaving him sitting there. She needed to move away from him before she lost it. Hopefully he'd just leave and go back to his hotel.

"I will do whatever it takes, Alex."

She spun around, fisting her hands at her sides, knowing she was losing control. "Let's get something straight. I adopted her. I found her as a baby and loved her as though she had been in my womb for nine months. *Me*. I did that. She is *my* daughter in every way that counts." All the tears she'd held onto were now streaming down her face, and she didn't care. He stood there, maybe an inch from her, and all she wanted was to prove to him that she was just as much a parent to Cassy as any biological one. But his handsome face was rigid, his jaw set, and he didn't show any signs of relenting. She took a step into him, swiping at her tears angrily. "I wanted a baby. I worked my ass off. No private school, no parents with deep pockets to help me out. I gave up university, college, all of it in favor of working as many hours as I could in order to save my money. The day I met that baby I knew she was mine. There was no parent who wanted her."

"I did," he bit out harshly, leaning into her. His face was fierce and he was all power and anger, so much that she wanted to move away from him. "I would have taken her the second she was born. I would have raised her. I had that privilege robbed from me. I had no choice, no say. I didn't even freaking know until a month ago. I have missed years of my child's life."

"Stop it." She covered her ears and squeezed her eyes shut. She couldn't listen to it anymore. She hated that she felt his pain and that everything he was saying was true. She felt his hands on hers, and a warmth seeped through her as she opened her eyes. His gaze locked onto hers and a shiver stole her words as she stood silent. Her breath was shallow and rapid as he dropped his hands from hers and instead moved them to frame her face. The pads of his thumbs wiped at her tears, but he didn't say anything. She had no words and part of her desperately wanted to push at him, to continue to yell at him, but the tenderness in his touch was disconcerting, soothing. If she leaned her head forward just an inch, it could rest on his chest.

"Alex," he said in a rough voice that sent a quiver down her body. "I'm sorry." He bent his knees slightly, and she opened her eyes to look into his. She stopped breathing, his face inches from hers, his blue eyes intense and filled with something so profound she wanted to both turn away and hold onto him for dear life. It was crazy, of course, to even think of holding onto a person that could ruin you. His gaze went from her eyes to her mouth, and his thumb slowly moved from her cheeks to beside her lips. Omigod, what was he doing? What was she doing? She backed up a step and crashed into the counter, knocking over dozens of stainless steel mixing bowls, the noise as jarring as fireworks in an enclosed space.

"I need a paternity test, Alexandra."

She backed away from him, relieved that whatever moment they had shared was over. She would forget this moment of compassion he'd shown her. Forget it. Lock it up and throw away the memory. He could go back to being her enemy.

He sighed. "Alex, I need to know if she's mine."

Of course she wouldn't let him go back to Vancouver without knowing. She wouldn't do that to Cassy, no matter how much it was killing her. She lifted her head and looked into those blue eyes of his. "I know."

"Why don't I stay here until you lock up? I can drive you home."

"I'm walking home."

He shoved his hands in his pockets and gave a rough sigh. "It's dark out. How far do you live?"

"A thirty-minute walk."

"That's too far. And it's cold and snowing."

"My favorite time to walk." Actually, she kind of hated walking. She was exhausted; the last thing she felt like doing was trudging through the snow all the way home. And she really despised walking alone at night. At least it was Christmas, which meant pretty decorations. The only reason she had been walking was due to her extra fifteen pounds of pastry weight that seemed to settle around her like a thick layer of fondant.

"Then I'll walk you home."

"I like walking by myself. It's a way to clear my head. I don't want to be forced to make conversation." She marched out of the kitchen and grabbed her coat and hat from the pegs on the wall. Hopefully she'd been rude and forceful enough that he would just leave. She got her keys ready and turned off the lights and walked to the front of the bakery.

"Ready to go?" he asked, shoving his arms into his coat.

"I think I was perfectly clear a few minutes ago when I said I was walking home alone. Now if you'll just leave so I can lock up."

"No. I'm walking you home."

"Why. Why *must* you walk me home? Why do you care so much?"

"You're the mother of my child."

"Ugh," she backed up a step. "Let's get something straight. First? She may not be yours. I don't care what this random one-night-stand woman claims. You don't know Cassy is yours. Second? I think it's kind of insulting, and... and....there's just something that doesn't sit well with you being fake concerned about me because I may or may not be somehow important to someone who may or may not be your daughter. And I don't think she's yours. I think that woman is a con artist and you're making all our lives miserable for no reason."

She could have sworn she heard him say, "what the hell" under his breath, but she wasn't sure. Instead, his face went a few shades darker, like she was really trying his patience or something. He took a few steady steps toward her. She crossed her arms and lifted her chin. If this was his way of trying to intimidate her, then it was working. Not that she'd ever let him see that.

He stood in front of her, a fierce expression on his handsome face. "Let me tell you something, Alexandra. I'm not here to ruin anyone's life. If Cassy is my daughter, there is no way in hell I'm walking out of this town without her. I will be a father to her. I will drag this through the courts if you don't cooperate with me. Hurting her is the last thing I want. I would think it's the last thing you want as well, so I suggest you cooperate with me."

Her heart pounded, as though it had swelled in her chest. Blood roared in her ears and pummeled through her body, and she was unable to find a voice, certainly not the strong, powerful voice needed to intimidate him back. She stared into his blue eyes, hating him. She hated everything he represented. She hated that his eyes were blue, just like Cassy's. She hated that he really might be Cassy's father. And she hated that he'd just threatened the only life she'd ever dreamed of. This was the life she deserved. She had lived through hell, and the only thing that had kept her going was this dream of one day having her own family, her own little girl.

"You can threaten me all you want. You can stand there and try and intimidate me, but you have no idea what you're up against, who you're up against. You may think I'm just this stupid woman who works in a bakery and you can come in here and take what you want, but that's not me at all. I bet I've seen more of the world than you ever have." Her voice shook and she didn't know if it was tears or rage, but it shook and it was low and it was raw. She didn't once look away from him.

"See you tomorrow. Cassy invited me to pick out a Christmas tree." He said it with a sense of victory, all amicability and charm gone. Now he was just this jerk of a guy.

She didn't say anything as he opened the door and left. She had no idea Cassy had done that. Her daughter was warm and trusting, and for some reason she had decided she liked Hayden Brooks. She was not going to overanalyze it... like Cassy maybe felt a connection to him.

She locked the door and shut off the lights, then she sat on the floor and cried, her body shaking. She hated confrontation; she never did well with it. She hated that he was right. He had a claim over Cassy if she was his biological daughter.

You get it together, Alex. Nothing has even happened yet. He might not be her father.

She stood, wiping her face and blowing her nose. The cold December air blasted against her face, as she made her way down the sidewalk. The walk was what she needed. Going home looking like a wreck would only make everyone worry. This would be a good way to blow off steam and forget about Hayden Brooks. She fell into a rhythm, her boots crunching against the snow. Usually she liked to take in the pretty houses with their Christmas decorations, the way the snow hung off tree branches, or the way the streetlights made the snow almost glow. Tonight she was deep in thought, barely paying attention to any of that. Who cared about things as silly as snow at Christmas time when her whole world was about to implode? Hadn't she had her share of misery? Hadn't she done her time?

Hayden Brooks was an ass. Those were her thoughts as she stomped up the steps of their front porch half an hour later. She paused, her hand on the doorknob as she heard the sound of a car engine. She turned around in time to see what looked like a black BMW drive off.

Hayden was standing beside his car, in Alex's driveway, cell phone at his ear. He was waiting for them to come out so they could go Christmas tree shopping. He knew it was their house, because he'd followed Alex home last night. Despite her pissing him off, he didn't like the idea of her walking home by herself. To further complicate everything, he hadn't been able to get her face or her voice out of his mind last night: *I found her as a baby and loved her as though she had been in my womb for nine months.* Something in him had shattered when he'd heard her speak. She loved Cassy with everything she had. She loved her more than her biological mother. He would rip her world apart if he took Cassy away. That was the only reason he'd tried to comfort her last night, the only one. He couldn't stand there while she cried in front of him. And the feel of her, the softness of her skin, her enticing scent…didn't have anything to do with it. It wasn't desire. The fact that he'd wanted to kiss her was purely out of…

"Are you even listening to a word I'm saying?" Ethan Dane yelled through the phone. His old university buddy and longtime friend was going through a hell of a problem and he was trying to help him out. He cut him off after a minute. "Ethan, my team is getting this done as fast as possible. As soon as their proposal is done, you'll have it. Besides, none of that even compares to the shit I have going on. I may have a kid, remember? Her mother hates me and basically told me she'd kick my ass if I tried to take her daughter." He paused and held the phone from his ear so he wouldn't have to hear his friend laugh. "Done? Not funny. I have to go. I'm going Christmas tree shopping to some place called blueberry something…what? You went there too? Why are you going to Christmas tree farms? Who's Spam? I'll talk to you later," he said as he spotted movement at the front door. "I gotta go."

Alex stepped out onto the front porch. She hadn't spotted him yet. Her dark hair was up in some kind of clip, and she was wearing a bright red coat and dark jeans. He didn't like that he noticed how pretty she was. Or that she'd made him feel bad after he got over feeling angry last night. She'd spoken to him with what had felt like barely controlled emotion. Her line about claiming to have seen more of the world than he ever had intrigued him, had sent a chill down his spine. He was getting the idea that there was much more to the woman who ran a bakery in a small town. He also knew that she had no idea how much Cassy meant to him if she were indeed his. There was no way he'd make a mistake a second time in his life.

He called out and she turned, her eyes narrowing as she spotted him walking up the driveway.

"Good morning," she said.

They were both spared having to make fake conversation because Cassy bounded out the door. "Hi! Are you ready to go get the tree?"

He smiled at her, that unfamiliar pull in his stomach happening again around her. "Can't wait. Are you ready?"

She bopped her head up and down enthusiastically. "Everyone's waiting for us to come back. Matt is coming over after to help us put up the tree and decorate it!"

"We can take our car," Alex said, taking Cassy's hand.

"I can drive."

"It's fine. I know the area."

"Let's go in Hayden's car! It looks so cool!" Alex looked away from him, but not before he caught the flash of anger or hurt. She stared at his car for a moment, her eyes narrowing. Why did he feel bad for her? He glanced down at her lips, which were just as full as he remembered from last night. Hell, he didn't feel bad for her. He felt bad for himself. Being attracted to Alex was not a complication he needed.

"That's fine," Alex said softly a moment later, leading Cassy toward his car. "We need to get the booster from ours."

A few minutes later they were pulling away, Cassy sitting in the backseat talking a mile a minute. Alex hadn't said a word; she was just looking out the window.

"Do you think it's going to snow?"

He glanced at Cassy in the rearview, smiling. She was wearing an adorable red hat with a pom-pom, a matching red scarf, and mittens. She also had on a snowsuit. He thought that was a little excessive, but what did he know about parenting. "I don't know."

"Do you like snow?"

He nodded. "I do. We don't get too much of it, but in the mountains there's lots, and I like skiing."

"You know how to ski? That's so cool! I'm going to learn how to ski. Mommy, can I take lessons this winter?"

He glanced over at Alex and her face went a few shades paler than normal.

"We'll see, Cassy."

"That means no," Cassy said, rolling her eyes. "Why do you always say no to cool things?"

Alex didn't say anything, but she was doing a lot of blinking. He didn't deal with emotional crap well. He hadn't been prepared for this. Nor had he been prepared for caring about other people's feelings.

"I don't think you need to worry about skiing now. So what are you asking Santa for this year?" He didn't really know how to talk to a kid, but he'd heard this question asked a lot during the holidays. He remembered people asking him this when he was a kid, and he really needed to distract her. He was starting to feel worse for Alex. Skiing was expensive and required time. He already didn't know how she managed with everything she had going on. Regardless of whether or not he liked her or the fact that she didn't like him, he wasn't going to manipulate Cassy in order to make himself look better.

"I'm still working on my list. So many toys, but my mom said Santa can't give more than two toys to every kid, because he wouldn't have enough for everyone."

He nodded. "That makes a lot of sense."

They drove, he and Cassy making most of the conversation the entire way. When they finally arrived at the farm, Cassy bolted out of the car and Alex grabbed her hand. "Parking lot rules. I know you're excited, but there are a lot of cars here."

Cassy nodded, looking up at him. She looked as though she was going to burst. She pointed to a big barn. "That place is the best. Are we going in there now, Mommy?" He looked around, taking in the rolling hills, the snow-covered escarpment in the distance. The air was crisp, fresh, and cold. It had a certain charm to it that even he couldn't deny. It also had the whole Christmas shtick down pat. Cedar roping, giant pots filled with greenery and hollies.

Alex shook her head. "After we pick the tree, we can go and warm up inside."

Cassy pulled on Alex's arm. "Do you promise we can go inside and get a treat when we're done picking our tree?"

Alex nodded. "Promise."

"Mr. Hayden."

"Hayden."

"You're going to love it inside. There are so many Christmas things. Decorations and gingerbread cookies and trees with lights."

"I do like cookies," he said, looking over his shoulder at

the barn that apparently was also a coffee shop, bakery, and store. He couldn't linger because Cassy was leading them through the tree farm adjacent the barn.

"We need to get the best tree ever! It's our first Christmas in Still Harbor so it needs to be extra special." Hayden and Alex followed Cassy as she marched with authority through the maze of Christmas trees. He'd never been tree shopping with a kid, and Cassy was all energy and bossiness. If he were reading into things, he'd say those might be personality traits she'd inherited from him. He didn't really know where they were. He'd just followed the directions Alex had given him. Apparently this Blueberry Hill Farm was renowned in the region. He didn't see anything that impressive but Alex and Cassy seemed thrilled to be here. He had no clue how or why his friend Ethan had been here, but considering how crappy his friend had looked the last time he saw him; it was no wonder he was ending up in places like this. It had taken them almost an hour to get here—he wouldn't admit that he thought driving an hour for a tree made no sense to him. He was still in the make a good impression stage. The car ride had been entertaining at least, since Cassy talked non-stop, which was perfect because it allowed him to not think about the woman sitting beside him.

They followed Cassy through the tree lot. The place was picturesque. Snow covered the hard ground and the escarpment in the distance was covered with snow as well.

"I think this is the extra-special section," Cassy yelled out from the top of the hill. Her voice carried as though she spoke through a megaphone. Very impressive. She had the makings of a corporate shark. Snow dusted the trees, and the ground was cold and hard, covered in white. He wasn't going to complain about it being pretty damn cold out here, especially since Alex and Cassy hadn't complained once. Vancouver definitely kicked ass when it came to winter weather.

They slowed when Cassy stopped suddenly and whirled around to face them, a massive grin plastered on her little face. The tree she was standing triumphantly beside was about five feet too tall for their house.

Alex coughed. "Um, Cassy, I don't think that'll fit in the living room."

Cassy frowned and perched her hands on her hips. "It will. You just need to believe."

Alex groaned. "This isn't about believing in miracles, sweetie. It's too big."

Hayden tried to diffuse the tension. "How about the one beside it? It's still big but looks much more manageable."

Cassy sighed theatrically and walked over to it, dragging her boots along the dirt. Alex was eyeing something behind the tree and then walked down a row. He didn't know which direction to go in. Tree shopping with two women was turning into something much more complicated than he'd envisioned.

"Wait! Cassy I think I found it, "Alex called out. "The perfect tree."

They walked over to where Alex was standing. She was beaming and holding the top of what had to be the saddest, most pathetic freaking tree he'd ever seen in his entire life.

Cassy screamed. "I'll die if that's our tree, Mommy."

Alex frowned. "It's so cute. He has character."

Hayden coughed and looked away from both of them. Damned if he did, and damned if he didn't. "It kind of reminds me of Charlie Brown's tree."

Alex crossed her arms and narrowed her eyes until they were squinty specks of green hatred geared toward him. "I kind of feel bad for it. No one will get it if we don't."

"Uh, yeah, because it's ugly! Why do we have to be the people with the ugly tree? I bet when Santa comes down the chimney and sees that tree, he'll run away screaming!"

Hayden knew he couldn't laugh out loud at the drama. He looked back and forth between them. There was something in Alex's eyes that tugged at his heartstrings, like this had to do with something else entirely. Something he didn't get, something that Cassy obviously didn't get. But he couldn't ignore it.

"What do you think, Hayden?" Cassy asked. She stared at him, her eyes like lasers. Crap. He was toast.

He stuffed his hands into this coat pockets. "Well, I guess it depends on the purpose of the tree…"

Cassy stomped her feet. He looked down. For a person with such small feet, they certainly made a big sound. "Mommy, it's supposed to be beautiful! That's the purpose."

He shrugged. "That's true."

Alex was shaking her head. "Nope. You have to like this tree for being an individual. If this is your tree, you have to love it even if the needles start falling-"

He had to interject in order to move this along. "Wouldn't you just water it more?"

Alex frowned at him. He wondered how he could find a woman who made tree-picking into a complicated event attractive. Extra attractive even, because he was actually intrigued by where she was going with this. "It's not as simple as that. Little trees can be very difficult."

"Look, if the tree is really bad, toss it to the curb and get a new one."

"Ah, well, I'll remember that," she said with a smirk.

He had a feeling this had nothing to do with a tree. "Get the tree, Alex."

"Noooooo," Cassy moaned and fell to the ground on her knees. Hayden looked down. He had no idea if all kids were this theatrical or if it was just her. He looked over at Alex.

Alex walked over to her. "How about this? We'll get your tree for the family room and my little tree can go in the kitchen."

Cassy nodded eagerly and sprang up from the ground. He breathed a sigh of relief.

"Okay, so I'll go tell the man at the register that we're taking both trees," Alex said, giving Cassy a kiss on the head.

"I'll get the trees. Why don't you meet me inside?"

"That's not necessary," Alex said, crossing her arms. "You'll probably be gone by Christmas."

He shook his head. "Nah, I'm pretty sure I'll still be here."

"Great! My mom makes all the food at our holidays and she's the best cook ever. You'll love it, and you can sit beside me if you want."

"No, Christmas is a long time from now, and I'm sure Hayden must have a job to return to."

He rolled on the balls of his feet. "That's one of the perks of running a company—you can take as much vacation time as needed. When needed, for important things."

Alex had turned from them and was smoothing the branches of her sad tree. Cassy went and stood by her tree, so he walked over to Alex.

"If I'm coming for Christmas dinner, I should definitely be buying the trees. Besides, I know the owner." So that was a bit of a stretch, but he knew, judging by what he'd seen of Alex, she would challenge him for the rest of the day and he'd be freezing his ass off trying to win an argument with her.

Her head snapped up. "*You* know the owner?"

Hayden nodded, grabbing the tip of the tree and yanking it toward himself. "His name is Spam."

Alex gave him a look that said he was full of it and tried to yank the tree back. He held on, but then she insisted on pulling it back. "I pay for our own things. I have always paid for Cassy, I don't need a stranger —"

"Possible father, you mean." He pulled the tree back so hard he took her with it. He caught her as she flew into him along with the stupid tree.

"Nice fathers don't go around shoving girls."

"I didn't shove you," he said, his voice sounding gruff to his ears. She was still holding onto him even though she'd regained her balance. He liked it. He liked the way she felt in his arms. He could feel her curves through her coat, and her voice was coming out in soft little gasps. Hell. Her mouth was open slightly and he knew he wasn't going to be able to resist kissing her two days in a row. Not this close, not when she was even more gorgeous close up. He dropped the tree and knew he'd rather hold on to her. Her green eyes locked onto his and he found himself…lost.

Until she shoved off of him and grabbed the tree. She gave him a wave, and a hot, shit-disturber smile and started walking off with the tree. She had played him. Thankfully, he was a helluva lot faster and taller. He caught up with her and yanked the tree back. He threw it over his shoulder and was about to give her the same smile she'd given him, when Cassy jumped out at him from one of the rows of trees almost scaring the crap out of him.

"Thanks, Hayden!" Cassy said and gave him such a giant hug he almost lost his balance. He didn't know what to do with the lump in his throat or the little girl hanging off him as though he were Santa Claus. He bent down and hugged her back properly, his heart filling up as she wrapped her arms around his neck.

"We'll go in and get hot chocolates," Alex said, breaking up the moment. He heard the strain in her voice, and when he looked up at her, she quickly turned away. She held out her hand to Cassy who took it eagerly as they made their way back inside.

He stood there, on the outskirts. They were family, Alex and Cassy. He was here, and even if he had the best of intentions, he'd be ripping apart the little family that they'd created. He could see them through the window. Cassy was pointing to something in the bakery window and Alex was shaking her head. Alex had been the biggest surprise of all. She was gorgeous. He found himself attracted to her, in a real, raw way. She lured him in, despite the fact that he knew she didn't trust him. He was here to take her kid away, and that knowledge was reflected in how she looked at him and acted around him.

She turned and spotted him staring at them. Something in his gut churned at the expression on her face. It was fear and vulnerability, and it made him uncomfortable. It made him question everything. She had taken in Cassy and loved her. She was the mother any little kid wanted. She was like his own mother in many ways. Alex broke his stare, but not before guilt railroaded into him. He owed her.

Chapter Four

They had made it back to the house with both trees. He looked around the family room with interest. The place had a warm, sweet vibe to it. It felt like women lived here. He and Matt were the only ones in the family room at the moment. Matt wasn't an easy one to figure out. He knew he was an ex-cop and now one of the best P.I.s in the country, but that was about it. Other than the fact that he was Kate's boyfriend.

His role here was interesting. He'd sort of taken on a protector role, and Hayden wondered about all of them and their connections to each other. Matt was protective of Alex and Cassy, and a part of him even appreciated that. They had been on their own a long time. Cassy could have used a guy looking out for her, a father. And Alex probably could have used the support. Even financially.

Matt was currently swearing and looking at the tree and then the instructions on the tree-base box. "Why doesn't this stupid base come assembled? And couldn't you have picked a smaller tree?"

"We did. That sorry looking one in the kitchen."

Matt grunted. "Alex."

He crouched down beside Matt. "How'd you guess?"

"Kate told me that Alex will not leave anything remotely sad behind. She's been after them to adopt a dog and cat from a shelter."

He didn't know why this information was interesting to him, but it was. He wanted to know more about Alex, and he was figuring out it had little to do with the fact that she was Cassy's mother. She interested him in a way that surprised him. She intrigued him. He'd never met anyone quite like her; she wasn't the type to run in his circles, and she openly despised him. That last part was one of the enticing things about her. He wasn't used to that. He was used to everyone liking him, women especially.

He was going to have to rein in whatever attraction he felt for her though. It would screw with his plans if he felt too sympathetic. Any kind of physical attraction was going to have to be pushed aside. He was going to have to stop checking her out whenever she walked by him. He was going to have to ignore everything he liked about the woman. He was going to concentrate on all the things that irritated him about her. That would do it.

"I have some new information about Cassy's mom," Matt said, lowering his voice.

Hayden gave the room a quick glance to make sure they were alone. "And?"

"Up until now, the tail we had on her didn't produce anything. This morning? She went to view a dozen or so million dollar plus properties with a realtor." Matt shoved the metal tree base at him.

"Shit." A surge of heat blasted through him. It wasn't a coincidence. "She's already making plans for her million bucks?"

Matt nodded. "Looks that way. What about the paternity test?"

"Next week I think."

Matt raised his eyebrows. "You got Alex to agree?"

He shrugged, remembering the conversation they'd had at the bakery. It had been heated, intense. He'd left with a helluva lot of respect for her because she'd stood her ground. He'd been surprised by his own lack of self-control, but he knew where this was all coming from. There had been another time in his life a woman had denied him any rights. He wouldn't ever let that happen again, no matter how hot Alex was. Or how vulnerable. Or sweet. He remembered the tree incident. So maybe not entirely sweet. "Not exactly, but I'm sure I will. I'm pretty convincing when I need to be."

Matt gave him a long look, and he almost expected to hear another warning, but after a minute he flicked his chin in the direction of the tree base. "Tell me you know how to put that thing together without having the tree fall over."

"I thought you knew."

"Hell no," Matt said, staring at the base. "All I know is, I said I was putting up a real Christmas tree, so I'd better do it. How hard could it be?"

The tree fell over three times before they dared called the women into the room. The little girls clapped as though they'd performed some sort of miracle. So did the women, except he suspected their enthusiasm was due to the fact they'd had no confidence in him and Matt.

"Now it's time for lights. Luckily for you guys, Kate puts the lights away every year so not one of them is tangled up."

Kate beamed proudly and handed out wheels of perfectly roped lights. "Since you two are the tallest, you can start at the top and I can delegate."

"I don't think we have that kind of time," Matt teased, giving Kate a kiss before grabbing one set of lights from her. The tough-ass persona Matt put on vanished whenever Kate and the girls were around. For them it was like he was a different person. Complete with sappy grin.

They hung the lights like pros. He kept his eye on Alex who looked like she was pretending not to be looking at him. Cassy stood at the bottom of the tree and gave them pointers.

"Matt and I have an announcement," Kate said. He turned toward the muted squeals, but when he made eye contact with Alex, she crossed her arms and looked away. He had no idea what was going on.

Matt wrapped his arms around Kate from behind, giving her a kiss on her neck. She visibly melted. He glanced over at Alex and Cara—they had visibly melted too—and so had the girls. He stared at Matt and couldn't figure it out. Sure, he was okay looking if you were into that kind of look. Tough, built, and...lovey-dovey. Huh. He never would have pegged that guy for being a sap. The first time he'd met him, when he'd walked into his P.I. firm, he'd been very aware of the level of testosterone and bad ass look he was giving him. He'd chalked it up to him being an ex-cop.

"Can I say?" Janie asked, looking up at them. He'd never been around a special needs kid before Janie so he didn't know what to expect. Hell, he'd never been around any kids, so Janie didn't seem that different to him. Matt hadn't seemed like a mushy type of guy, yet he'd found a way to bond with these kids.

Most of the time he didn't really think about the kinds of people he dealt with in business, in life. News stories filtered in and out of his brain, sometimes having an impact, never lasting. When you were a single guy, wealthy, without any kids, things could bounce off you easier. Something was happening to him here — things weren't bouncing off. They were sticking and evoking different emotions in him. He hadn't thought about work all day. He hadn't thought about the hotel. Nothing. He had been consumed by Cassy…and Alex.

"Yes, you can," Matt said, looking at Kate who was nodding.

"I'm going to have a daddy," Janie said. "Him," she added, poking Matt in the stomach. He picked her up, grinning as Alex and Cara ambushed Kate, laughing and hugging her. Hell. It felt weird being here, at a moment like this, with people he barely knew, yet could become unbelievably important to him.

Cassy looked at him as she hugged Janie. Then he glanced over at the woman he was most curious about, and he went still. He made eye contact with her and read the longing, felt the longing, and a second later she was looking away from him.

Man, none of these people were what he expected. He didn't even know people like this existed. They were good people. In a world fully of shitty, horrible, self-serving people, they were proof that other people existed. They had all formed some kind of family, but now he was here, threatening to destroy it.

"How about I make us some hot chocolate?" Alex asked. The girls screamed out, and Alex gave the most convincing smile she could and walked to the kitchen. She was happy to get out of that room. Matt and Kate, it wasn't a surprise. They had all known this was coming. The second they'd stood up there, she had known. It should be impossible to feel so happy for someone while at the same time being very aware of how much your own life sucked. Kate and Matt were the real thing. He was the real thing, and Kate and Janie deserved a guy like him.

Then there was Hayden. Hayden looked as though he belonged there. And all the girls looked completely comfortable with him. Cara and Kate looked as though they liked him. Matt looked as though he approved. So it was just her. She reminded herself she didn't have to like him. She could be civil and that's it, except for her other inconvenient feelings. He turned on the charm. It was obvious he was only doing this to get her to let her guard down. Well, he wouldn't fool her. He thought he could just lay on the charm, and she'd melt in his arms. No way. Almost, but, no way. She added some milk to the pot and waited for it to simmer. She took down the marshmallows and washed a pack of strawberries.

"Need any help?"

She looked up and fumbled, a bunch of strawberries falling into the sink. Hayden was leaning against the counter as though he owned the place, as though he'd been doing this kind of thing forever. She frowned, upset at herself for noticing how good he looked. He looked different from the night he'd arrived at the bakery. Then he'd been all business, handsome, corporate… Now he was casual and equally appealing. Hayden was one of those irritatingly, naturally good-looking people. His hair was kind of messy, but on him it looked slightly delectable. And speaking of delectable, the stubble across his jaw only enhanced his features. Then there were the eyes, and the way he looked in his navy sweater and worn jeans that made it very obvious the man was ripped. Of course she now knew he was solid and hard under his clothes because she'd ended up in his arms two days in a row, that bastard. She snapped the plastic lid off the second pack of strawberries, sending them tumbling into the sink.

"You sure I can't help?"

Ugh. His voice, when he wasn't demanding a paternity test, was deep and sometimes tinged with a little bit of softness. She squared her shoulders and told herself to focus. "Uh, no. Thanks. I've got it under control."

He ignored her and joined her at the sink. His large hands brushed against hers as he helped her collect the berries. His arm was pressed against hers and she suddenly found it impossible to breathe. Or think. Until the sound of the forgotten milk bubbling over shoved her from her thoughts. Hayden beat her to it and was there in a second, pulling the pot off the stove. "I happen to be an expert hot chocolate maker," he said, a smile in his voice. She lined up three mugs on the counter ignoring the smile. "My mother made the best hot chocolate."

Past tense. She should ask if she was still alive, because it sounded like she wasn't. But she didn't want to know about his personal life. She also didn't want to hear that he'd had a good relationship with his mother. He wanted him to be this jerk ready to ruin her world. She did not want to like him. She did not want to notice him. She didn't want to think he was attractive. No, not only attractive, but maybe *the* most attractive man she'd ever met. She also did not want to acknowledge that she was sucking in her stomach, because that would be stupid.

"Your tree looks good in the kitchen."

She could have sworn she saw his lips twitch slightly and would've laughed if he were anyone else. She was starting to like him; she hadn't counted on that. He was kind, sweet even. And patient. So much patience. He was so sweet to Cassy. He answered all her questions. He listened to her talk non-stop while eating cookies and in the car ride home.

He even made sure she got her Charlie Brown tree. It had also been a pleasant surprise how much she liked having a guy around. It had always been just her and Cassy. They'd never had a guy around them. She hadn't dated. Ever. She'd always been on her own, and she never trusted people. She'd never even been tempted by guys. Sure, she acknowledged good-looking men. She'd been there the night they'd hand-picked Matt for Kate at the bar. But she hadn't ever wanted someone for herself. In all her life plans, getting married hadn't made it on her to-do list. Her list has been occupied by things like, oh, survive, find a job, save money, start a life with Kate and Cara, adopt a child, build a home, be stable.

Also, she had planned on living alone after Cassy left. She was fine thinking of her sisters getting married while she was a modern-day spinster. Sex was surely highly overrated. Same with marriage. Who needed to worry about someone else all the time? Why would she want some guy demanding things of her?

Or maybe she was just chicken. Maybe she didn't want a man rejecting her. Maybe she didn't want him walking out on her one day. Would he tell her she was too bossy? She was too fat? Would she want a man telling her that marriage wasn't for him and then abandoning her? She didn't need that. She needed the family she'd built and nothing more. A man like Hayden wasn't a family man. He didn't even live in the province.

He expertly stirred in the cocoa. He pulled the pot off the stove and poured the hot chocolate into the waiting mugs. She couldn't stop staring as he used his left hand. Why hadn't she noticed this before?

"Something wrong?"

She shook her head and then looked up at him. "Are you left handed?"

He gave her a nod. "Yeah."

She tore her gaze from him and looked down. She was not going to freak out. It didn't mean anything, even though as soon as he left she was jumping on Google. "It's nothing."

"It's something," he said, walking closer to her, too close. Way too close to hide.

"Cassy's left handed," she whispered, her chest heaving with the knowledge of the very real possibility he was her father. "Let's…uh, let's do the paternity test."

She walked out of the room, not waiting for his reply, not wanting to hear his voice, to be in his presence.

Alex took a deep breath and tried not to stare at the strange comb-over Mr. Tuttle had going on. It was closing time at the bakery and he'd graciously accommodated her schedule and had come to meet her here instead of at the bank. She, in turn, had supplied the man with giant pieces of pie and hot chocolate.

Alex glanced at her watch and took a deep breath. Time to concentrate. She rifled through the papers spread all over her table and then looked at her computer screen that had her bank balances displayed. There was no way she could do this. She had money saved, but not nearly enough. She wracked her brain for another way to get some extra money or a bigger line of credit while Tuttle ate. She refused to even think about using her credit cards. Besides, the bank would figure that out, and it would be irresponsible.

She eyed her car keys on top of her purse and stopped breathing for a second. What was her car worth? Not that much, it was used. But it wasn't old. Maybe she could get ten thousand for it.

She took a deep breath. Yes, she would look up the blue book value of her car, print it out, and show it to Mr. Tuttle if he turned her down today. She didn't need to have a car to get around Still Harbor. They were walking distance to most things. Cara and Kate both had cars so even in a bind she could use theirs. Great. She would list the car tonight for sale.

She tried to look confident and relaxed, as though asking for a small business loan in the hundred thousand dollar range was something she did on a daily basis.

"The Sweet Spot Bakery is practically a landmark in Still Harbor. We have an established clientele, business grows each year, and I have years of experience. I've spent my entire adult life in the bakery business in one form or another. It's really risk free for the bank," she said after he inhaled the last bite.

Mr. Tuttle nodded repeatedly as he wiped the crumbs from his mouth.

The appearance of a familiar and irritatingly attractive-male figure in front of the bakery window momentarily distracted her. Hayden Brooks was standing outside but not looking in their direction. He was on his phone, and by the looks of the things, and the puffs of breath, followed by the distinct mouthing of a four-letter word, his call was dropped. It was a regular occurrence in Still Harbor. The jolt of satisfaction wasn't something she was proud of, but she felt it nonetheless.

He turned around suddenly, making eye contact with her. She wrapped her hands around her coffee mug, trying to look casual and not at all like she was taken aback by her immediate reaction to him. She was obviously deprived of hot-man contact. Sure Matt was hot, but he was now like a brother to her, so he didn't count. Tuttle was the only other man she'd had a longer than five-minute conversation with, and he didn't seem to evoke the same reactions. Hayden Brooks was not a man she needed to be feeling any attraction to. He gave her a wave and she returned it, saying a silent prayer he'd keep on walking past her window. She tensed, sitting up in her seat as he opened the door. Ugh. This was the worst time for an unscheduled visit.

Tuttle was completely unaware of the new person in the shop and started talking again about how strict the criteria was. She sucked in her stomach as Hayden glanced over at

her. She sat a little straighter in her seat and nodded seriously as Mr. Tuttle kept on talking. She motioned with her hand
to keep his voice down and darted her gaze in Hayden's
direction.

Mr. Tuttle's mouth opened into a theatrical O. "Yes, we
don't need customers worrying that anything is going to
happen here."

She breathed a sigh of relief, but she needed to finish up
this meeting. She needed the bottom line here.

"So, all of this is to say, my dear, that at this time I don't
think we can offer you a loan."

She didn't blink, move, or even release the breath that
hopefully made her abs look like a washboard. She was
vaguely aware of Hayden's gaze on them but refused to look
over. She leaned forward and kept her voice low and calm.
"Mr. Tuttle, I have an *established* clientele."

"I know that, my dear, but your debt load ratio would be
too high between the mortgage on your current home and
then the business."

She knew she wasn't the type to cry in public, never had
been. She'd had disappointments. She'd had her share of
rejection. But in the last month alone everything that had
been a sure thing was now up in question: Cassy and the
business. She covered her face for a moment and leaned
back in her chair. She hated that two men were watching
her. She removed her hands and forced a pleasant expression on her face.

"Well, Mr. Tuttle, what can I do to convince you to give
me a small business loan?"

His face went red and she could tell he hadn't expected
her question. He sighed deeply, while packing up his laptop

and papers. "You need more money, that's the gist of it."

"I have more. I just didn't tell you about it."

She named a safe figure she'd be able to get for her car and prayed while he winced.

"I'm not sure."

"Don't say no yet."

"Excuse me, miss?"

Alex frowned at the interruption. Really, Hayden needed to order food right this minute? She plastered on a polite face and turned to him. He was standing at the register, a Rudolph cookie in his hand. Seriously, he was interrupting her for a Rudolph cookie? "I'll be with you in a minute, *sir*." And that was the other thing, what was with the miss?

"Actually, I'm in a hurry. I'm here to place an ongoing corporate order if you have the means to provide. I'd be looking at regular monthly orders of cookies, muffins, and croissants. Regular catering for our offices. Very large volume."

Her mouth dropped open, and she didn't move. He just stood there, beautiful eyes on hers, a force, a presence in her store. He was doing this for her. Even Mr. Tuttle stopped moving for a moment, then he leaned forward and patted her hand. "Why don't you go work out the details of that business and get back to me in a few weeks to see where you're at, dear?" He gave her a wink and left the store. She still sat with her butt glued to the chair. Hayden was now leaning against the counter and had bitten off Rudolph's head.

She stood, walked to the door, and locked it behind Tuttle. It was closing time anyway, and she needed a moment to process what had happened.

"Thank you," she said, walking over to him. "I mean, you totally didn't have to do that."

He shrugged. "My company is far, but I have a couple good friends who have a company in downtown Toronto. I'm sure they'd gladly sign you on for regular corporate events."

She busied herself with packing up the leftovers. She couldn't allow herself to get lured into this rescuing a damsel in distress thing he was toying with. It was fake. To get points. All of it was about Cassy. If Cassy wasn't his, then all this extra business he was promising would be gone. "You don't have to do that."

He splayed his hands wide on the counter. "Why not? You needed a loan."

She continued packing up the cookies and not looking at him. "It's fine. I'll find another way. It's generous of you, but when Tuttle figures out it's a lie—"

"I'm not lying. I can get you corporate accounts."

Her mouth dropped open, and then she shook her head.

"You don't want my help. If it were Matt standing here, you'd take his help."

She slammed the glass door on the refrigerated cabinet shut and glared at him. "Matt isn't trying to take away my little girl."

He ran a hand over his jaw. "Speaking of, when did you want to do the paternity test?"

Her mouth dropped open. "That wasn't a very smooth transition."

He shrugged. "You shoot down all my attempts at being nice. I thought I'd save us both time and be direct. The other night you told me you were ready, but you're avoiding doing it."

She lifted her brows. "Fine. It's been really busy between work and the Still Harbor House we're working on. You know, not all of us have extended, month-long vacations. I have to go over to the group home and help out. Matt's been there, pulling in tons of hours, and we need to help out more."

"I can help."

Her eyes narrowed slightly. "Thanks for the offer, but—"

He leaned against the counter all smooth, panther-like grace, so not what she needed to see right now. "You don't want help? You don't need help?"

"It's not that."

"Ah, so you don't want _my_ help."

This man was persistent. "Well, there isn't some executive's office that you can bark out orders from to employees."

His firm mouth twitched slightly at the corners. "Because that's what you think I do? Yell out orders from some large corner office?"

She shrugged. "Maybe. Probably."

Now he grinned a full-on sexy grin. "Well, as much as I like the image, I do much more. And I know my way around a construction site."

"I guess you've managed to learn a lot from the backseat of a limo when you power down the windows."

"Again this image of the high-powered executive that you've probably seen in Hollywood movies."

She held up her hand. "I don't get my opinions from Hollywood."

"Oh, of course not. Just from the other executives in town, like Tuttle?" The grin turned into a full-on laugh that was rich and deep, and completely contagious. So, she was baiting him, and she'd fallen for her own bait because the man was downright charming. He wasn't even the least bit put-off by her attempted character insults. Huh. "I grew up on construction sights. My dad would take me with him when I was little. When I was a teenager, that's where I'd work in the summers, not the office. I built my own house, along with a crew. So, maybe I can actually be of use."

Ugh. So he was even more impressive than she'd previously thought.

"I'll help you lock up and then we can drive over to the group home."

She knew there wasn't any point arguing with him. "Fine, but I'm walking."

"That again."

She would have said that for someone who was in such good shape, she'd expect him to like the idea of walking. She didn't say that, of course, because that would mean admitting she noticed the way he looked.

"Well, you can drive."

"I'll walk with you."

"So, walking…in the snow. This is fun." He thought he heard a laugh, but when he looked over at her, she wasn't smiling. They had been walking for almost fifteen minutes in complete silence. He had been processing everything he'd overheard in the bakery. She was trying to buy it. She had no money. It's not that he was surprised. No, what surprised him was his own reaction. He'd felt for her. He wanted it for her. Regardless of what would happen between them, she deserved her own place.

"When you work in a bakery, you have to sneak in every opportunity to burn off the inevitable calories that you ingest during the day. I go in with the best of intentions, but there's always something to try or sample. I've put on fifteen pounds in the last year," she said. He glanced over at her. She looked perfect to him. He didn't see anything that needed to come off. He knew he was treading on dangerous ground though when it came to women and weight.

"You could always try running."

Wrong answer. Her eyes were all squinty and evil as she looked at him again. "I wasn't asking for diet advice."

Diet advice? "What? No, that's not what—"

"No, it's fine."

None of it would ever be fine ever again if he didn't get this sorted out fast. "You're misinterpreting what I meant. You said you gained fifteen pounds. All I'm saying is that running burns lots of calories and—"

"You think I need to burn lots of calories."

He was so up shit's creek. "No, I'm not saying that."

"You did. You *just* said that."

"We need to back this up. Right now. For the record, I think you look normal."

She threw up her hands. "Great. I'm glad I don't look like the horrible, obese monster that I was imagining."

"You're hot, Alex. That's what I would have said if I'd thought it appropriate. You're hot. Your curves are in all the right places, and I find that incredibly attractive. But I'm not supposed to say any of this because of our situation. If you were anyone else, anywhere else, things would have happened."

She didn't say anything. He glanced over at her, and he could see her cheeks were slightly rosy. The glower had lessened, and he assumed he'd fixed the situation. Close call. But she stopped talking and she stopped walking. He stood in front of her and her eyes were circling all around like she didn't want to look at him. "It was the curves in all the right places remark, wasn't it?"

She rolled her eyes. "Please. I know hollow compliments when I hear them. It was the 'things would have happened' remark. That crap doesn't fly with me and it perpetuates the whole millionaire exec in the limo image I have of you. Besides, it's stupid to worry about fifteen pounds. I'm not worried at all."

"Sounds like you're worried."

"I have bigger things to worry about than fifteen pounds. Maybe if I didn't, maybe if my life had been slightly more normal, I'd worry about that. There are people out there, suffering, dying, grieving, just trying to survive. The bakery that I have been saving up to buy is now no longer an option for me. Some man who is claiming to maybe be the father of my daughter is about to wreck my world. Those are real problems. Fifteen pounds? I really couldn't give a damn."

Shit. She wasn't vain or self-indulgent or self-interested. And there was that mention of her past again. He took a step closer to her. It was so stupid, standing this close to her, because this close up he could see how green her eyes were. He'd been mistaken that first night, when he thought they were the color of cedar roping. No, they were a deeper, darker shade of green and filled with so many secrets he felt like begging to know just one of them. Her skin was flawless. Flecks of snow clung to her dark hair as it fell around her shoulders. Her lips were perfectly shaped and she didn't have an ounce of anything on them. They were full. Plump. Luscious. And that got him thinking about her body. Good God, he was way too attracted to her.

She shoved him. "No. You can't try and be charming now. I won't fall for it. It's your attempt at trying to get me to lower my defenses. Not working. You're the guy who wants to take away my daughter. You're the enemy."

"Mommy! Hayden! Hurry up!"

She backed up a step from him and turned to a red brick house. Cassy was jumping up and down on the front porch. He waved, trying to look normal. He needed to get it together. His lawyer would kill him if he found out he'd tried to pick up the woman he was going to battle for custody against.

"Coming," Alex called out and then ran ahead of him. He followed her, and Cassy gave them both big hugs. Seeing Cassy every day this week had been the best part of his visit. Every morning at the inn he'd use the gym, then check in with his office back in Vancouver. Late afternoon he'd head over to the toy store and ask the woman behind the counter what a popular toy for a six-year-old girl was. Then he'd stop by their house and give it to Cassy and spend some time with her. Luckily it was always Cara at home after school so he didn't have to worry about pissing Alex off.

"Come inside," Cassy said, yanking his sleeve. He shot Alex a look, but she plastered on a hollow smile and followed them in.

"Okay, so this is going to be the new shelter?"

"Do you like it, Hayden?" Cassy was looking up at him with that toothless grin that always made him smile back without even thinking.

"I do. Do you want to give me the tour?"

She nodded rapidly and held out her hand. He took her small hand in his, that squeezing in his heart surprising him again. He wondered if he'd always feel that way when she held his hand or if it was only because now all of this was so new. "Come this way," she said, dragging him with a surprising strength.

Alex was looking at them, her face pale. Her smile looked forced as she stood there watching them as they left the room. Cassy led him around the first floor, pointing out the family room, the kitchen, the mudroom, and the small office. She pointed out all Matt's handiwork and then the one wall she and her sisters had painted. "Now, the upstairs is still in rough shape, but it's getting there." She marched up the stairs with authority. "So the moms get their own rooms and so do the kids, unless the kids want to sleep in the same rooms as their moms. That's nice, don't you think?"

He nodded. "Makes sense."

She pointed to the first room. "This room is my favorite because it looks at the backyard. Come here, look out this window." She yanked on his arm, and he followed her to the big bay window. It was an impressive view. The backyard was covered in snow, but there were large trees; the yard was picturesque. "See that fountain? It's not running, just has a rock wall right now. But Matt made that for my Auntie Kate. Nice, don't you think?"

He nodded, looking at the fountain. It was an odd kind of gift.

"Because she had a mom once and they used to make wishes at a fountain."

They didn't say anything for a long moment. "I had a mom." The lump in his throat, the one that always appeared whenever he thought of her, was back. He wondered what she'd think of him now, with this little girl beside him, the girl that could be her granddaughter. He cleared his throat, forcing all the emotion away.

"Not anymore?"

He shook his head.

"I'm sorry to hear that," she said, taking her hand in his. Then she patted it. He looked down at her, and she was staring up at him with this earnest face, big blue eyes that seemed to see something in him. "My mom is Alex. And I love her."

"Hey, guys? Cassy gave you a tour of the place?" Alex was standing in the entry, and he turned to her, seeing the expression on her face, reading the insecurity there. He didn't get what was happening to him. All these feelings... and shit. It was all the women around constantly. They made him think about...things besides work. Hell, he had no idea how Matt survived like this.

Cassy tore away from him and did some kind of skipping run over to Alex. "Yup. Are there snacks downstairs?"

Alex nodded, ruffling the top of Cassy's head. "Yup, and Sabrina is coming over to play with you girls." Cassy jumped up and down. He already knew that Sabrina was Matt's younger sister. More women.

"Bye, Hayden! I think my mom's going to make you work now."

Cassy left before he could reply. Alex walked into the room, and he found himself checking her out. She'd taken her coat off and was wearing a red sweater and dark jeans.

Her dark hair was pulled up in a ponytail and she looked ready to work. And she looked hot. He was noticing the curves he'd mentioned before.

"So what can I help with?"

"You don't have to help at all. You could go back to the inn."

He ignored her. "What can I help with? Matt mentioned some baseboards need installing?"

She nodded, and he could tell she was kind of disappointed he was staying. "Yeah, they're in the next room. I'm going to paint the trim. You can go ahead and start doing that. Matt said his toolbox is in the next room. Help yourself to whatever. He'll be by after work."

"Great."

He walked by her and caught the scent of vanilla. He picked up his pace and got the hell out of the room.

An hour later, Alex poked her head in the room. "How's it going?"

He finished another board and sat down on the hardwood floor. "Good. Should be done soon."

She nodded, her gaze surveying the room. She looked like she approved of his work. "Dinner will be here soon. So um, can I ask you something?"

He nodded. From where he was seated he had a great view of Alex. She was kind of dishevelled now. Her hair was messier. Her sweater had a splotch of paint on the front, right above one very nice, very full breast. He tore his gaze away when she crossed her arms. "Go ahead."

"Did you, um, do you keep in touch with the woman who is Cassy's mom?"

He shook his head.

She walked a bit closer to him. "So you don't really know anything about her."

He shook his head again. "Are you trying to find out more about her?"

She rolled her eyes. "Of course."

He shrugged. "I can't tell you much."

She pursed her lips. "Because it was a one-night stand."

Hayden put down his hammer and looked up at the woman currently pretending to ask an innocuous question, when in reality he knew it was fully loaded. "Yes."

"Do you think she's lying?"

He shrugged. "Yeah, a part of me thinks she's lying. A part of me thinks she may believe…the baby was mine."

"You never saw her again?"

He shook his head, wondering where she was going with this. "That's the biggest perk of a one-night stand—you never have to look at the person again."

"But…if it was good, wouldn't you want to see her again? Unless it wasn't good."

He choked on his own saliva. "I'm not answering that question."

She crossed her arms.

He shrugged. "It was all right, as far as one-night stands go. You know how it is."

She made some sort of remark under her breath that made it very clear that she didn't like his answer. "No, actually I don't know."

"Never?"

She frowned at him and shook her head.

"I find that surprising."

He told himself to maintain eye contact at all costs and

to not get lured into her appeal. She was setting him up, and he needed to remain focused on their conversation and not her…assets. "What exactly do you mean by that?"

"I mean that usually a person has one or two of those in their history by the time they get to a certain age." He picked up his hammer again and tried to make it look as though he was concentrating on the baseboards and not on having a night with Alex.

"Well, not everyone has the luxury of free time. Or deep pockets to spend at a bar… Also I haven't arrived at a certain age yet."

"You're lucky. You're a woman. One-night stands usually don't cost you anything. Just wait around for a guy to buy you a drink."

"What wonderful advice. Be sure to jot that down in a book of notes so one day when Cassy is all grown up, you can tell her that."

He swore as he almost hit his finger with the hammer. He decided to set it down again and look up at Alex. She was giving him the best evil eye he'd ever seen. Her hands were perched on her hips, and her sweater was stretched tightly over the finest breasts he'd ever seen. The glower emanating from her eyes forced him to look up again. "Fine. You win. You're all wrong about me anyway. You're making rash decisions and judging."

She held up a paintbrush hand and waved it around. He moved quickly to the left to avoid getting splattered. "Not at all. I'm not judgmental in the least. Perhaps if you were… someone important to me…as in a romantic sense, I'd care a little more. But you mean nothing to me. You mean some-thing to Cassy, maybe. Maybe not."

He stood close to her, deciding he didn't need to listen to the sensible Hayden that was telling him to back it up from the woman. He liked the way she looked flustered the closer he got to her. "See, I get the feeling you're trying to piss me off. Maybe try and come up with this flawed personality sketch of me. Maybe a reckless playboy who drinks and parties too hard? Then if the paternity tests come back and Cassy is mine, if we have to take this through the courts, you can tell them all about my horrible behavior?"

She lifted her chin and pursed her lips. "My sole objective is to make sure my daughter is safe and happy and loved. You are implying that I'm trying to be devious. Really, I was only asking a personal question. I wasn't coming up with some underhanded plan."

He didn't believe her. Truth always disarmed people, especially if the truth was the exact opposite of what the person expected. "That was the only one-night stand I've had in my life. It was a rough time in my life—the anniversary of my mother's death and another event in my life that I never speak of. I was at a bar, feeling shitty. I drank too much, went to a hotel with this beautiful woman, used a condom, and that was it. I didn't see her again for seven years."

Alex's gorgeous mouth was hanging open. The paintbrush was dangling by her side and there was a sheen in her eyes. He took another step toward her, telling himself to play it cool; he was winning this round.

"I, um, I'm sorry," she whispered. "I'm sorry about your mother and whatever else happened to you." Then he stood there as she reached out to hug him. He felt the paintbrush against his back. He felt her soft body against his as he held her.

She pulled back abruptly. "Also, I'm sorry because I had been secretly praying that you might hit yourself with the hammer."

He could still feel her body against his, even as she left the room. He was floored by the emotion he saw in her eyes when she'd said she was sorry about his mother.

She had won the round, he realized.

Chapter Five

"That tasted kind of funny," Cassy said.

Alex plastered a smile on her face, even though she felt like crying. She placed the swab back in the airtight, sterile container and sealed it. There. Done. In a week they'd know if Hayden Brooks was Cassy's father. She chose to ignore the slight guilt she felt at not waiting until tomorrow to do the test with Hayden, as they'd decided. "Well, it's all done."

"Do you think there's something wrong with me? Is that why I needed to do that test?"

Alex shook her head. "Not at all. Just making sure your throat infection went away." Alex quickly shoved the contents of the kit back in the box and placed it on one of the upper bookshelves in the family room. She'd deal with shipping it to the lab tomorrow.

"What happened to our car, Mommy?" Cassy asked, sitting with her on the couch in front of the Christmas tree.

It was one of those rare nights where the house was empty. Kate and Janie were at Matt's mother's house. Cara and Beth were out Christmas shopping. So she and Cassy had decided to read some books and sit and enjoy the Christmas tree. Now that the paternity testing was out of the way, she could relax. Or try to.

She smoothed Cassy's hair and kissed the top of her head. "Well, I was thinking it would be great for us to get lots and lots of walking done. We don't really need a car since we live so close to everything."

Cassy's face turned downward and into a frown. "But I like our car, Mommy."

Alex ignored the pang of guilt she felt. This was for their own good, an investment for the future. It would give her the security she craved so deeply. She had sold the car last night to someone in town, a nice couple looking to buy a safe car for their son who was commuting from home to college. It was a solid chunk of cash she could put straight into the bank and hopefully toward the Sweet Spot Bakery. "We'll get another car soon, okay?'

Cassy moved back from her slightly. "But it won't be *our* car."

"A car is a thing. It can be replaced. We can't replace people but we can replace objects."

Her heart swelled when Cassy put a smile on her face and leaned forward to give her a hug. "Okay, Mama." Cassy only called her mama on rare occasions. Alex squeezed her to her side. "Love you, Cassy."

"Love you. Also I was thinking maybe Santa might get us a new car."

Alex laughed. She couldn't argue that logic. "Let's not

get our hopes up though, okay?'

Cassy nodded. "I like Hayden, do you?"

Alex stiffened slightly. "He seems like a nice man."

Cassy turned so that she was now facing her on the couch. "He also smells good."

Alex frowned. "Pardon?"

"Yeah, I like how Matt smells nice. Men smell different from women."

Alex tried not to groan. How was her daughter noticing this stuff? She propped her feet on the coffee table and stared absently at her reindeer-print flannel pajamas. Why was Hayden making this impression on her? Oh, maybe it was because he was making this impression on everyone, not just her daughter. Just the thought of him made her break out in a cold sweat, and not all of it was because of the possibility that he was Cassy's father. Part of it was this awful... impossible reaction or attraction she had for him. Like when he'd basically handed her a bunch of corporate contracts in order to help her appeal for a loan, or when he was helping out at the new group home and had gone all seductive. He'd been capable and giving, and downright sexy. She had hung around in the doorway, drooling as she watched him work, the play of muscles, the bulge of biceps, the efficiency and ease with which he worked.

"Mommy, are you listening? The way Hayden smells?"

Hayden smelled delicious. Like cedar and winter. Or maybe just hot man.

"Hello? Mommy?"

She smoothed Cassy's hair away from her face and kissed the top of her head. "I hadn't really noticed."

"Also, I think that it's nice to have a new friend here

for the holidays. Maybe he could be your boyfriend, like how Matt was Auntie Kate's boyfriend. Now they're getting married. That would be nice for you, don't you think?"

Alex's mouth dropped open.

"It worked for Auntie Kate."

"Well, it doesn't just work like that. It's special to have something like Auntie Kate and Matt. It doesn't just happen with anyone."

Cassy bolted off the sofa, hands on her hips and faced her. "But it can happen. Why don't you try smiling at him?"

Alex blinked. "I smile."

Cassy rolled her eyes. "Only when he's not looking! Try smiling *at* him! Or maybe you can bake him some cookies or something."

This could almost be funny. Almost. Except that it was really, really sad. Her six year old was giving her pick-up tips. "Sweetie, it takes more than that. I can't bribe someone with cookies. You can't fake love or buy love."

"Well, then do more. Hayden's so nice, and you're cranky to him."

Omigod. "I'm not cranky. I'm just busy. Hayden is on… vacation. He's doing nothing, just bumbling around Still Harbor, so of course he's going to be more relaxed than I am. Besides, we don't need someone else in our lives. Are you not happy just you and me?"

Cassy nodded and toyed with the hem on her snowman flannel pajamas. "I am. But it's just that I got to thinking how nice it is in the house when Matt is here. Like, he does silly things. And he picks us up and throws us around. I thought that was just Matt, but then Hayden started hanging around us and he's as silly as Matt. Yesterday he even pretended to drop me when he held me up to look at the Christmas tree. It was so fun. So I thought Auntie Kate could keep Matt, and we could keep Hayden. "

Alex put her head in her hands and groaned. "Oh, Cassy."

"Maybe he could be a dad, and I'd have a dad like Janie's going to have one."

She dropped her hands. She knew where all this was coming from, but it still hurt. It hurt to feel that she wasn't enough, that she wasn't doing enough, when every day she gave it her all. "You know not everyone in the world has a dad, right? I mean look at Beth and Auntie Cara, there's no man for them. We'll be fine with the four of us."

"But that means that Auntie Kate and Janie will be moving out. Then it'll be lonely around here."

"First off, there will still be four of us. Second, Auntie Kate and Matt and Janie will be here all the time. We're always a family. We don't have to live together to still be a family."

The doorbell rang, and Cassy ran to it. She was already squealing, and Hayden's deep voice filled the entry by the time Alex got to the door. Her heart sank, and unfortunately her pulse raced at the sight of him. Cassy was hanging onto his leg; he had a bag in one hand. His hair was all mussed up again. He was already taking off his coat like he'd been coming to their house for years. He had on a navy henley and dark jeans and looked better than any damn cupcake she'd ever baked. Or eaten.

She folded her arms in front of her. "I didn't know you were coming by tonight. It's Cassy's bedtime. I was just about to tuck her in."

He flashed her a grin, which basically told her he didn't really care. "I was at the bookstore in town today and spotted a bunch of Christmas books I thought she would like," he said and handed Cassy the bag.

"Thank you!" Cassy threw her arms around his waist and she stood there, feeling a bit more of the life they'd created slip away from her. Hayden's deep chuckle filled the entryway and the two of them stood there, looking so much like father and daughter that her heart ached and it hurt to breathe.

"Can Hayden tuck me in? Maybe he can read me a book?"

"I don't know, sweetie. I'm sure he has something to do. Rumor has it that Hayden has a job. Maybe he needs to go to work."

"Nope. Taking a vacation, you know that. First one I've had in years, so I'm good with tucking her in."

Alex threw up her arms. "Fine. Then by all means."

"Okay. I need to talk to you after I tuck her in," he said, moving toward her.

"Fine." She walked toward Cassy and gave her a big kiss.

"Goodnight, lovey."

"Night, Mommy."

She stood at the bottom of the stairs and watched as Hayden and Cassy made their way up, Cassy's chatter trailing down as they moved away from her. She gripped the banister, squeezed her eyes shut, and prayed her daughter wouldn't be taken away from her.

"**G**ood job. Great read, Hayden."

Hayden laughed, closing the book.

Hayden had settled in beside Cassy on her bed. He stretched out his legs as best as possible. He'd already finished '*Twas the Night before Christmas* and was now sitting and talking with her. He knew Alex had been pissed that he'd just shown up on their doorstep, but he didn't really care. He wanted to make sure the paternity test would be sent out tomorrow. Enough stalling. He needed to move forward, and he also needed to get back to work. He also needed to get his attraction to Alex under control. The woman could wear a bag and look hot. Even her reindeer pajama pants, wet hair, no makeup, and disgruntled expression were the hottest thing he'd seen this year. Next to the red tank top thingy she wore with spaghetti straps and cleavage…and he also knew that she felt as hot as she looked because of the hug she'd given him. She'd completely disarmed him. He hadn't expected that…compassion. And he hadn't expected the jolt of desire.

"I never had a dad before."

Hayden turned to her. Hell. He didn't know what to say, but he did know that he was a man unaccustomed to tears or emotion. Things didn't really phase him, but she did. Her little hand in his did.

She looked up at him, those blue eyes locking onto his so he didn't dare look away, not that he would. "Janie has a dad now. Matt. He's not her real dad, but he's good enough."

"Yeah, Matt's a cool guy."

Cassy nodded. "Sometimes people don't have to be pathological to be family."

He tried his damndest not to laugh out loud, but hell. "I

think you mean biological."

She nodded again, like it was just a minor detail. "Like, Janie and Beth aren't my real sisters, but my Mom said that blood doesn't have feelings and feelings make family."

He cleared his throat, thinking of Alex, and all the ways she had impressed him. Every single time she annoyed him, she still managed to impress him. And then he thought of that night in the bakery when he'd lost it and she'd yelled at him, telling him bluntly that she was the first person to love Cassy. "Your mom's a smart lady."

She nodded again. "That's probably why I'm so smart."

He grinned. Hell, whenever Cassy said something like that, he knew it didn't take a paternity test to prove she was his; this kind of arrogance was in the genes. "That makes sense."

"She works so hard, Hayden."

He knew that. He thought of the day at the bakery with the oaf from the bank. He felt her desperation, her panic, and it bothered the hell out of him that someone like her needed to struggle at all. "I know she does."

"She sold our car to some family."

He closed his eyes for a second. The loan. She was putting money toward that bakery.

"Oh, don't feel bad. We can use Auntie Cara's car. My mom already told me."

He cleared his throat. This all mattered to him so much more than it should or more than he would have expected. "Yeah, that's true."

"You know my sister Janie?"

He nodded.

"She has Down's Syndrome. That makes her different

from us, but that isn't a bad thing. Different people are special. Janie is special in different ways than me and Beth. We look out for her. Sometimes she has a hard time doing things, so we help her. My mom says we should help different people and when we treat them extra kind, we're also being extra kind to ourselves. We learn how to be patient and to be better people."

He stared at the little hand in his and for the first time since he was a kid, said a prayer.

He prayed Cassy was his. He wanted in on this, this life they were living. The last life he'd ever have contemplated for himself was now the only one he wanted, except he wasn't going to live this life with them. He was going to do the exact opposite. He was going back to his life, back to work, across the country and he was going to take her with him. He was going to take her back to make his father happy, to chase some kind of memory of his mother, to help himself from his own demons in his past. He wanted to prove he could do this, that he still deserved to be a father after everything he'd done. Hell. "Your mom is right. Again."

"Yeah. You know what happened at school?"

He shook his head.

"Everyone was sliding down the giant snow piles that the plough makes in the school yard. Janie was too scared to slide down so this mean boy in our class shoved her down because he was tired of waiting in line. Janie cried."

"That wasn't nice of him."

"Nope, it wasn't. So I told Beth to help Janie, and I walked up to him and smashed a pile of snow in his face."

He wanted to high-five her, but he didn't know if that kind of behavior was acceptable so he just raised his eyebrows and waited for her to continue her story.

"I yelled at him. I told him that he'd get double that amount of snow in his face if he ever bothered my sister again."

"What did he do?"

"Well, by then Beth had brought the playground supervisor over. We both had to go into the principal's office."

"And?" This was the best freaking story he'd heard in weeks.

"I explained my story, and she took my side but told me I shouldn't do that again. He had to stay inside for recess for a whole week."

He was damn proud of her. "Janie's lucky to have sisters like you and Beth."

"That's what Uncle Matt said. But first, I heard him talking in the kitchen with my mom and Auntie Kate and Cara and I heard him say that he was going to bash that kid's dad's face in next time he saw him."

He burst out laughing. He wanted in on this family thing they had going on. He wanted the crazy, the funny, the love.

Cassy's eyes widened. "It's not funny. Auntie Kate yelled at him for saying that. He promised he wouldn't."

He nodded, trying to look serious again.

"So, are you staying for Christmas? Did you decide?"

"I'd like to if your mom says it's okay."

"I'll put in a good word for you."

He laughed again. He was always laughing with Cassy. "Our moms make it a really fun Christmas. And this is our first Christmas with Uncle Matt. He makes things fun. He can be silly. Way sillier than our moms. Kind of like you. I heard our moms saying it must be a guy thing."

"Do you eavesdrop a lot?"

She looked slightly mortified. "It's the only way to get any reliable information."

He squeezed her hand.

"Now that Auntie Kate and Uncle Matt are getting married that means Janie gets a dad."

"Yup."

"And that means they are going to move out."

"Yeah. Sometimes thing change in a house."

She nodded, looking wise beyond her years. "I don't think I ever want to get married. My friend Samantha always likes playing married games with her Barbies. And she talks about things like getting married. I think it's stupid."

"Getting married?"

"Yeah. I won't have time for it."

He didn't want to smile and have her think he was making fun of her. "So what will you spend your time doing?"

"I'm going to be a captain."

He was proud. "That's a fine profession."

"Yup. Captain of my own pirate ship."

He wasn't going to burst out laughing. Hell, no. He was going to pretend that wanting to be a captain of a pirate ship was a perfectly acceptable profession. And if he remembered correctly, there was a point in his life where he thought the same. "Do you know where you're going to sail?"

"Depends on what treasure maps we find." She tossed him a look that suggested she doubted his intellect; obviously their route would be determined by the treasure map.

"Wouldn't you miss your mom and sisters?"

She shrugged. "They could totally come with me. But I'd have to be captain." She shot him a sidelong glance.

"Maybe you could come on my ship. Help out below decks or something. If you're still around."

His laugh was quelled by the sudden sadness that crept into her sweet voice. If he was still around… "That would be nice, captain. Ever hear that expression, work like a captain, play like a pirate?"

She shook her head.

"My dad said that to me one day. I had made a pirate ship on their bed, because they had a king-sized bed and I thought it would be cool to set up a sail from the big four posters. So after my dad came home from work that night, he brought up a plate of cookies and two glasses of milk and sat on the ship with me."

"That sounds like fun," she said, staring at him with those big eyes. He felt himself drawn back to that time in his life, when everything had been perfect. He rarely visited that place, but Cassandra made him want to for some reason.

"It was. My mom made the best cookies."

"When did your mom die?"

He frowned. "When I was ten."

She moved her head and rested it on his shoulder. He felt the weight of her head against him, and his heart squeezed. "I'm sorry that your mommy died."

He cleared his throat. "Me too, Cassy."

"Do you still miss her?"

He nodded. "I do, especially around Christmas. She really loved Christmas."

"Well then maybe it's good that you're spending Christmas here. My mom makes delicious cookies. Maybe I'll tell her about your mom and that you love cookies. I'm sure she'll bake you some."

"You have a good mom, Cassy."

She nodded against his shoulder. "Yup, I know. I'd like to have a dad one day. Would you like to be a dad one day?"

He stared up at the ceiling, the stars glowing brighter now. "I think so." His voice came out sounding hoarse. More than anything right now, he wanted to be Cassy's dad and he wanted to build a pirate ship. And he wanted to wear an eye-patch.

Shit, he was done.

"Well. That's good, because I see the way my mom looks at you."

He wanted to stop this conversation and yet he wanted it to go on forever. He could listen to this little girl all day long, he realized. She was clever, sharp, and very endearing. Her earnestness killed him. She was also extremely astute. He cleared his throat, bracing himself. "How does your mom look at me?"

She paused for a moment, a little frown appearing on her forehead as she shifted to look at him. "She smiles at you when you're not looking. Sort of like she's staring off into space. It looks silly, because no one is smiling at her, but she's smiling at you and you don't even see."

The damn lump was back in his throat.

"I don't know if you know this, but she's not my pathological mother."

"Biological."

"Right. But she loves me just like a pathological mom. Well, more than a pathological mom, because my pathological mom didn't keep me. So that makes me think that a dad, even if he isn't a pathological dad, would love me just as much."

He squeezed her little hand in his. "I think anyone who marries your mom would be privileged to be your father. And I know for a fact that they would love you so much and they'd never leave."

She nodded. "I hope it's you," she whispered.

He needed to shut this down before he revealed something or made a promise he couldn't keep. "I think I was supposed to tuck you in a half hour ago," he said, standing. "Wanna know a secret?"

She nodded, her face brightening.

"I have no idea how to tuck someone in."

She thought this was hilarious. "But you're a grown up!"

He smiled. "Yeah, but I've never tucked a kid in before."

"Okay," she said smiling and sitting up on her knees. "What you have to do first is make sure I'm under the covers."

"Got it." He helped her slide into the pink and white striped sheets.

"Next, cover me up."

He pulled the covers over her head and laughed as she squealed.

"Not over my head, silly!"

He drew them back down, smiling at her. She was looking at him as though he were the best man on earth. It was humbling. "Like this?" he asked, tucking them under her chin. She nodded, still smiling, anticipating another bonehead move he was sure. He tried to think of something so he could hear her laugh one more time but couldn't come up with anything. He just stared at her, thinking how perfect she was with that toothless grin.

"Now you have to give me a kiss, turn out my light, ask

me what I'm grateful for today, and then that's it!"

"What you're grateful for?"

She nodded. "We all do that, every night. Our moms said it's a nice, positive way to end the day and remind us of all the things we are grateful for."

"I think that's a great idea."

He leaned down to give her a kiss on the forehead.

"What were you grateful for today, Cassy?"

"You."

Chapter Six

Alex paced the family room, waiting for Hayden to come back down after tucking Cassy in. She was not feeling threatened at all, even though the sound of their laughter trickled down into the foyer. Usually bedtime didn't bring a lot of laughs around here, yet Hayden had been able to do it. She had to tell her daughter they didn't have a car anymore, while he was up there giving her daily presents.

She stopped pacing and stood there as she heard him tread down the stairs.

"Hey," he said, standing in the doorway. "She's all tucked in."

Alex nodded, ignoring how good he looked standing there in his jeans and shirt. Fabric clung to him in a way that was not fair. She also knew, thanks to her ridiculously impulsive hug, that he was all hard lines and muscle. And Cassy was right, he smelled delicious. Why she had given him a hug, she'd never know, except he'd looked vulnerable when he talked about his mother. A tenderness had appeared in his blue eyes, the lines on his face had softened, his shoulders had dipped slightly; and standing there with that mussed up hair…she hadn't been able to resist reaching out to him.

It wouldn't happen again, even though she kept replaying the conversation on their walk, the one where he told her that her curves were all in the right places. That was just another charmer line from a man that could charm this entire household.

She crossed her arms, suddenly self-conscious in her pajamas as he walked toward her.

"Nice music," he said.

She moved away from him, picking up a throw blanket and wrapping it around herself. She didn't need him analyzing any curves of hers. She didn't like her reaction when his gaze flicked down to her tank. Nope. Satisfied when she was finally covered like she was ready to face a polar ice storm, she answered his question. "It's the Alvin and the Chipmunks Christmas album."

He gave her a nod, his mouth hitching up at the corner slightly. "Nice. Listen, I wanted to ask you about the paternity test."

She eyed the spot on the bookshelf. "All done."

He frowned. "I thought we were doing that together."

She shrugged. "I thought I'd get it done and over with. I know you're in a hurry. I thought I'd do you a favor."

He gave her a level stare. She straightened herself up when he walked toward her. She had no idea how he could walk around with that kind of authority when he didn't even own the house. "So you'll send it back tomorrow?"

"Yep. I'll add it to my list of errands. I won't be around

tomorrow."

"Day off?"

She nodded. "I was planning on going into the city to get Cassy this toy she's been asking for all year."

"That's perfect. I'm heading into Toronto to meet some friends. I can drive you."

"No thanks, I'll just drive myself."

"You don't have a car."

She pursed her lips. "I was going to borrow Cara's."

"That doesn't make sense. If I'm going there anyway, just come with me. Unless…you don't want to be in a car with me for over an hour."

She crossed her arms, but then the blanket fell. He trapped her, the SOB. His eyes traveled the length of her body, and she scrambled to pick up the blanket even though she now felt like she was on fire. That look…it was like the look she gave a cupcake before devouring it. "No, that's just silly."

"Great."

"But you're not coming shopping with me."

"I'd rather die."

"Still…I plan on leaving first thing in the morning."

He gave her a flat look. "I'm a guy. If you want me here at eight, I'll roll out of bed at seven forty-five, shower, and be here for eight. It takes me ten minutes to get ready."

So unfair. He could go around looking that good. He probably woke up looking that good. In fact, he was probably the type that looked even better when he just woke up—mussed-up hair, scruffy face, heavy-lidded eyes. She cleared her throat. "Fine. Come and pick me up at eight."

He gave her a nod and walked toward the door.

"Nine!" she called out.

He nodded, and she could have sworn she saw a small smirk before he opened the door and left.

What was she thinking? She was going to spend the day with the man that she was supposed to hate but now was actually starting to like? She locked the door behind him and walked back into the living room. She pulled down the box with the paternity test and hugged it to her chest.

She needed to remember who he was, and what he'd do to her if Cassy was his.

At exactly nine a.m. Hayden's BMW pulled into the driveway. He was punctual. Normally that would be a good thing, but this man was all good things so far, except for the fact that he wanted to take her child away from her. She made her way to his car, pulling on her gloves as the wind turned bitter, whipping snow around as though it were powdered sugar. The inside of the car was warm and toasty, and she could smell his cologne or aftershave or whatever it was that made him even more appealing than a second cup of coffee this morning. Cassy was right; he smelled delicious.

"Ready to go?"

"Yup," she said, buckling her seatbelt.

They were on the road in minutes, and she gave him directions to the highway. "I hope this snow doesn't get worse," she said softly, trying to relax in her seat.

"I'm sure it's nothing."

"This from the guy who lives in a place where it rains instead of snows in December."

He cracked an adorable grin that made her look away. "I head up to the mountains too. I understand snow. And I went to college in Toronto. I remember the crappy weather around here."

"Well, snow at Christmas beats rain any day."

"Sure, unless the snow is so bad the roads are closed."

"That rarely happens. Like, hardly ever."

He had the good manners not to argue. "So what are you looking to buy Cassy for Christmas?"

She stared out the windshield, the taillights the only thing lighting up the dull gray sky. "I don't know what I'm going to buy her. I just want to get her something special this year. The places we have around us don't really have anything unique." She wanted to buy her daughter something special because she loved her…and she was insecure. It was pathetic. She knew Cassy wouldn't love her anymore than she already did because of the toy she bought her for Christmas, but she was aware of all the material things Hayden would be able to provide her. She had worked hard at building a secure life, taking charge, building a family filled with unconditional love. But now Hayden was here and threatened to ruin all of it.

"Who are you meeting in Toronto?"

"Some of my old friends from school."

"You still keep in touch?"

He nodded. "Yeah, and my company is working on a proposal for one of my friends."

"What is it?"

"A condo in the downtown area."

She nodded. "That's nice of him to ask you."

"I'm the best, and he's very aware of that."

Omigod, the arrogance. He wasn't even cracking a smile, just driving with one hand on the steering wheel, one hand on the gearshift, and his eyes steady on the road.

"Does your friend actually like you?"

He laughed. Rich, low, deep. Ugh. "Yeah, of course. We get each other. All four of us."

"There are four of you running around?"

"Well, technically Jackson is married now. He doesn't do anything except show people pictures of his wife and kids."

She smiled. "He sounds nice."

He gave some sort of grunt. "Not that long ago you could say he was the biggest asshole. But now—"

"You are?"

She said it with a smile without even thinking about it. He laughed. And dammit if her insult didn't make her like him more. It was that laugh. Like he was so sure of himself he didn't even care she was insulting him.

"No, no, it's Ethan for sure. That condo proposal we're doing for him? It's so he can shut down a youth homeless shelter."

She gasped. "That's awful. Disgusting."

He shrugged. "Especially because he's in love with the woman who runs it."

She shrieked. "What kind of people are these? I'm scared to ask about the last one."

"Nicholas? Nah, nothing special about him. Just a boring lawyer."

She settled back in her seat.

"So what time do you think you'll be finished?"

"Well, I want to get all my shopping done today if it's possible. So maybe six o'clock?"

"How many people do you know?"

She laughed. "Just the girls, Cara and Kate, and Matt. Oh, and Matt's mother and sister. It will be a miracle if I get it all done today."

He turned to her briefly. "You're kidding?"

"Ask anyone, it's a big challenge to do all that in one trip."

"I'm not asking anyone."

"Well who do you shop for?"

He paused. "Just my dad…and this year, Cassy."

It was disconcerting to think that Cassy had already gotten used to him. Hayden was now someone she looked forward to seeing. "Just um, drop me off and pick me up at six. I'll be waiting."

He didn't say anything for a long moment and then nodded.

"I think we should have left a few hours earlier," Alex said peering through the windshield. The snow was coming down so hard that even the wipers on the highest setting weren't doing a good enough job.

"We'll be fine," Hayden murmured, not looking uncomfortable at all.

"You're only saying that because you have no idea how bad driving conditions can get."

"You know, I do have access to television where they show snow storms."

She glanced over at him, not appreciating the sarcasm in his tone. "I bet you that this highway is going to be shut down in the next half hour."

"It won't."

Of course, as they kept driving at a slow pace, Alex counted each car they passed that was in the ditch. "I really think we need to get off the road."

"And go where? We're in Nowherseville."

"Maybe we can take the back roads home."

"And get there by Christmas if we're lucky?"

"Fine, then what do you suggest?"

Alex gasped and held on as she felt the car slide. "Omigod."

"It's fine. Everything's under control," Hayden said in a calm voice. She could tell by the concentration in his eyes and the clenching in his jaw that he didn't think this was fine anymore. He swore and then quickly tried to steer the car to the left as the tractor-trailer beside them veered into their lane. "Okay, we're getting off," he said after they were safely away from the truck. Alex didn't move, just kept gripping the hand rest between them and trying to get her breathing under control.

Hayden efficiently changed lanes, and they made their way slowly to the off-ramp. He swore under his breath, and she gasped at the amount of cars that had slid off. Police cars with lights flashing were scattered around. "I hope no one is seriously hurt," she whispered.

Hayden didn't say anything and she stopped talking, letting him concentrate on the road ahead. They both breathed a sigh of relief when they reached the end of the on-ramp.

"Okay, do you have any idea where we are?" he asked her.

She shook her head. "Some small town. It's really dark,

though. It's hard to see anything."

He ran his hands over his jaw as he waited for the light to change. "I guess our best bet will be to get into the downtown center, which is…somewhere."

Fifteen tense, long minutes later they made their way into the center, which consisted of a bank, a general store, a gas station, and a Tim Horton's coffee shop. Hayden pulled over onto the deserted street and looked at her. "We gotta find somewhere to stay overnight."

She looked out the windows. "Where?"

"I'm going to look up our location and find the nearest place."

"Good luck."

"No choice. We're not sleeping in the car."

Five minutes later he looked at her with dread in his eyes, his mouth pulled down into a frown. Unfortunately, he still looked good, maybe even better than before. Maybe it was his lack of panic. "So we're officially in the village of Brighton, which means we are in the middle of nowhere. There's a B&B a few blocks down the road. What do you think?"

She shivered and pulled her coat closer. He started the car again and pulled out onto the road, blasting the heat and directing the vents in her direction. She mumbled out a thank you and refused to acknowledge to herself that the man was actually sweet. The road off the highway was winding and colossal snowdrifts had formed. He had to veer into the opposite lane to get by.

"I guess no snowplows are out in the rural areas yet," she said softly. He didn't say anything and she knew he was concentrating on getting them to the B&B safely. The roads were so bad she didn't even have time to be upset that they weren't going to make it home tonight.

"What the hell?"

She turned to see what he was looking at and gasped, torn between covering her eyes and looking out the windshield. An eighteen-wheeler was barrelling down the hill, in the opposite lane, blaring his horn. The way the truck was sliding, he was going to encroach on their side of the road. "Oh shit, hold on," Hayden said.

Don't scream, don't scream, don't scream.

She screamed as she felt their car veer off the road, sliding, spinning and then finally stopping with a thud that jerked her forward. She opened her eyes and only saw white.

"You okay?"

She turned to Hayden. He looked fine. He looked pissed, but otherwise unharmed. She nodded.

"That moron basically ran us into a drift."

She looked out the windshield; that explained the white.

"I'm going to get out of the car and see how bad it is," he said. He was outside before she could even reply. She took a few deep breaths and calmed down. They were fine. Maybe she should go outside and help. The door opened a second later. Hayden, followed by a gust of wind and a blast of snow, entered the car. "We're not going anywhere."

"What do you mean?"

"Well, the car isn't going anywhere, not until they plow the roads and I can shovel us out. There's no point now, because new snow keeps piling up and the wind is so strong that it keeps blowing around existing snow."

"So what are we going to do?"

"Walk."

"In this?"

He looked at her and she found herself irritated that he wasn't more upset. Hello, they were basically trapped in a car, were being forced to stay in the middle of nowhere, and now had to walk through a blizzard.

"It's not a blizzard, just a snowstorm. Besides, this Sugar Plum Inn isn't too far."

"Maybe if we just stay here—"

"We can die?"

She frowned at him and crossed her arms. "I feel the need to point out that this was a poor choice of a rental car."

His perfect jaw tightened. "Excuse me?"

She nodded, lifting her eyebrows. "Yes. I mean this foreign car is incapable of handling the winter."

"I only drive imported." The way he said it made her sit at attention. She was finally seeing Hayden behaving less than pleasant and she liked it.

"Well, it's hardly a family-man type of car. You should have rented a mini-van." She paused as he gagged. "Or an SUV. None of this would have happened."

"At least I *have* a car."

Her jaw dropped open. Sure, she'd been openly baiting him but that was a low blow. She expected him to apologize. Instead, he muttered something under his breath that didn't sound apologetic at all and then opened the door and left the car.

She sat there for a moment, stunned, until panic set in. Was he going to leave her here? It was pitch black out, and she had no idea where this Sugar Plum Inn was. He would leave her here because she had been nasty. He was going to walk off, and she was going to have an anxiety attack. She

falling for her enemy

knew very well she had issues being left behind; she should have apologized. She should have been smiley and complimentary and then he wouldn't have—

His head ducked inside the open door. "Are you going to get out of the car soon? I'm freezing my ass off."

"I thought you were gone," she whispered, horrified that tears were stinging the back of her eyes. He frowned and she caught the exact moment where he thought she must be insane.

"Where the hell would I go? As if I'd leave the mother of my kid sitting in a snowdrift. Let's go." With that he shut the door. She was just going to be grateful at not having been abandoned. She was not going to allow herself to be insulted that he'd basically said the only reason he wasn't leaving her here was because she was Cassy's mom. And she wasn't going to point out that Cassy may not be his.

He whipped open the door again, his hair all white with snow, and a nasty look on an incredibly handsome face. "When I said I was freezing my ass off a few minutes ago, I meant it."

She nodded, quickly unbuckling her seat belt, grabbing her purse, and joining him outside. She took giant steps to round the car, careful not to lose her footing and end up in the drift like the car.

"So, according to this," he said holding up his phone. "Sugar Plum should be only a five minute walk from here."

"Wait!" she yelled as he started walking.

His sigh was actually louder than the wind. But he waited.

"I need to get my shopping bags."

"We're not carrying your shopping bags."

"I refuse to leave them here. What if someone smashes into the car, or steals or—?"

"Fine. Hold on. Then we walk fast."

She nodded agreeably and didn't say anything as he grumbled with each bag he pulled out of the back seat. When he got to bag number eight, she heard him curse.

"I'll carry them, Hayden," she said, reaching for the bags. He shrugged her off and marched down the road.

Icy, grainy snow whipped across her face as she followed Hayden. He kept a really fast pace considering the snow and wind and all the bags, but she knew she had to force herself to keep up. It was freezing and there was no time to dawdle. She threw her purse strap over her shoulder and concentrated on following Hayden's footsteps. If she kept her head tilted downward, she avoided the wind in her face. The snow was coming down so fast, though, that his footsteps were disappearing almost instantly.

The idea of being inside a quaint B&B on a stormy night was becoming more and more appealing. She could set up a nice hot bath, maybe step into a spa bathrobe, and then rest in a giant four-poster bed. She even picked up her pace at the thought. The B&Bs she saw in magazines looked so fabulous, almost like a five-star inn and spa. Even the name The Sugar Plum made her envision a roaring fire in a Victorian fireplace, maybe some homemade cookies and hot tea placed on an antique tray in the sitting room. See, she was capable of being positive, despite the fact that they couldn't make it home during a blizzard, and that she was with the man who threatened to ruin her life. Nothing was going to get her down. Alexandra McAllister was not a downer. She was a fighter.

"Holy shit."

Alex bumped into Hayden's back and then slowly moved to his side to see what had caused his outburst. She inhaled sharply and then tried not to cry. A sign was swinging off a small pole, and she was pretty positive it said THE SUGAR PLUM. Except because of the snow, and the missing letters, the only letters still intact read, THE S-L-U-M. That was putting it mildly. Even though she was chilled to the bone, she stood still taking in the sight of the decrepit two-story house. It was Victorian all right. Except it looked as though it hadn't been touched since the day it had been built. Shutters hung on their sides, the eaves trough was falling on one side, and the wooden front door was chipped, paint peeling. Giant icicles clung to the eaves, and two of the porch lights were burnt out. Overall the place had a total horror-movie vibe.

"Omigod, *this* is the Sugar Plum B&B?"

"No," Hayden said grimly. "It's The Slum B&B."

"What do we do?"

"We have no choice. There's nowhere else to stay in this dump of a town," he said looking down at her. She nodded and they made their way up the front steps. "Careful," he said, pointing to the block of concrete that was loose. He knocked on the door, and she stood close to him, realizing that he blocked out a lot of the wind.

Minutes later the door creaked open and the scariest-looking man she had ever laid eyes on answered. He was a few inches taller than Hayden, had long black hair, and was wearing a black tank top. His eyes were darker than his hair and they seemed to want to burst out of his face.

"Lost?"

Hayden shook his head. "Our car is stuck in a ditch. We're looking for a place to stay for the night until the roads are plowed."

"Well, we only got one room."

She tapped on Hayden's shoulder. He ignored her.

"That's fine, we'll take it."

"Five hundred dollars."

She gasped and tapped on his shoulder again.

He ignored her again. She leaned up and hissed in his ear, "You're getting hosed, pretty boy."

He turned to look at her, and she had no idea if his expression was shock or rage, but he didn't say anything and turned back to the man. "I'll give you two hundred."

The man nodded eagerly and held out his hand. The door opened wider and they walked through. Alex glanced around the foyer and wanted to weep as the warm, albeit slightly smelly air, greeted them. It must have been a beautiful home when it was built. Deep trim and mouldings lined the entry. A grand staircase with a thick, mahogany banister and rail trailed the graceful flight. Unfortunately, dust and grime had attached to the wood, and none of it gleamed anymore. The rugs were threadbare, and the paint on the walls were faded and stained. She glanced over at Hayden who was currently counting bills and placing them in the man's outstretched palm. He had that kind of cash on him? She would have to talk to him about paying her half once they were in their room.

"Follow me," the man said and started marching up the stairs.

Hayden motioned for her to go first. She shook her head, and he rolled his eyes following the man she would now silently refer to as Igor. They followed Igor down a long, dark hallway. She counted at least six closed doors. "You folks are lucky I have a room left." He paused in front of a narrow door and she prayed that their room wasn't really a closet. He opened the door and took out a stack of white linens. "Bobby-Joe, my wife, is staying at her Cousin Marla-Jean's house."

"Of course she is," Hayden said under his breath.

"Which means there are no clean sheets on the bed. So if you like that sort of thing, here you go," he said, and thrust the pile at her. Alex stumbled back a step at the weight of the towels and sheets. She was going to bite her tongue and not say anything about the fact that the lazy oaf could have put the sheets on himself, instead of blaming it on poor Bobby-Joe.

"Thanks," she said, following as Igor started walking again. He turned a corner and stopped at a closed door. "Here's my last room. Third floor. Hasn't been used in a while."

"That's surprising."

He ignored Hayden again. "But at least that means it'll be clean."

"Wait!" Alex called out. "Is that the attic?"

Igor nodded.

Alex shook her head. "Nope. No, I can't sleep in an attic."

"Missy, this ain't the Ritz."

"The attic is fine," Hayden said, shooting her a look. She forced herself to calm down. She backed up a step and into Hayden. He was a hard wall of...something hot and comforting.

"Nope."

"Alex."

"Missy, that man is holding all yer shopping bags. I don't think this is the time for antics."

Hayden stepped in front of Igor to block him.

"I don't do attics," she gasped.

She could tell he was about to say something sarcastic but then his features softened. "You can. Nothing's going to happen. I won't let anything happen, okay?" Maybe it was the tenderness in his deep voice that made her feel safe, or the protectiveness in his eyes. She looked back at Igor who seemed spookier than ever looming over Hayden's shoulder. *Do not panic, Alex. You won't be by yourself. It's not really an attic if it's all finished. It's just another room.*

Igor handed Hayden an old-fashioned key and started to walk away. "Oh, I should probably mention not to worry if you hear any tapping or footsteps during the night."

Alex didn't move, didn't process what Igor could possibly be talking about.

"What do you mean?" Hayden asked, as Igor walked away from them.

"It's just old Patrick McGee. Rumor has it he died in the house and never really left," Igor said with a nonchalant shrug.

Alex inhaled sharply and reached out to clutch Hayden's arm. He looked down at her, clearly puzzled by her reaction.

"We can't stay here. I don't like ghosts."

Hayden laughed, then stopped abruptly when he looked into her face. "Alex, there are no ghosts here. Seriously, Igor over there— "

She inhaled sharply. "You think he looks like Igor too?"

"It's his *name*. Igor Plum. I saw it on his business card."

"Omigod. Shut. Up," she whispered. "I can't handle this. I'm getting a very weird vibe here."

"Of course you are. This place is a dive, he looks like he's out of a horror movie, and he just warned us about some Irish ghost. Listen, there's no ghosts here, just some guy who's dipped into the spirits for the night."

"Bad pun," she whispered as he fiddled with the key.

He smiled. "I'm quick on my feet." He leaned down and picked up the bags, holding open the door for her. She peered through and saw only darkness. She shook her head.

"I can't do this. Here's the thing, I am normally quite self-sufficient—"

He nodded seriously, but there was a glimmer of something sparkling in his eyes that suggested he questioned just how self-sufficient she was. "But there are a few things I don't do well with." She lifted up her index finger, ready to give a count when he interrupted.

"How about I turn on the lights and go first. You can follow."

Clearly, he had no interest in hearing about her. That was fine. His way was probably more efficient. He locked the door behind them and then fiddled for a light switch, bumping into her before finding it. A dim light lit the entry and she found herself standing inches from Hayden. He paused there for a second, an expression passing over his face before turning back around and making his way up the long staircase. The stairs creaked with every step, and she was somewhat relieved they didn't look too filthy. They reached the top of the stairs and both stood still, taking in their surroundings. It could have been worse. A large bed with a worn brass frame was in the center of the room, flanked by iron and glass mismatched bedside tables. An old purple velvet chair sat in one corner of the room. A white dresser took up the other wall. All in all, it was a hideous room. The only reason it didn't seem too bad was that she had expected much, much worse. She had also anticipated it activating some memories that she'd worked hard to bury, but this looked nothing like the place in her memories. This was different. She was different. She was an adult. She was with another adult. It was fine.

"Okay, looks like the bathroom's in there," Hayden said, walking over to peer inside the open door. "It looks... passable," he said, turning back around. He dropped the bags and she placed the stack of linens on top of the dresser.

"I should probably try and call home," she said, fishing for her phone in her purse.

"Good idea," he said, unbuttoning his coat. She watched him out of the corner of her eye while she waited for someone to answer. He was rubbing his hands through his hair, shaking off some of the water and she let her gaze wander over him, now that he wasn't watching her. If he were not the man who was currently trying to rip apart her life, she would consider this the universe's way of giving back to her for the years of solitude she'd endured. But alas, no. This beautiful man was actually the universe's way of making sure she would once again have her security, her loved one, abandoning her. This man—she swallowed as her gaze wandered over the broad shoulders, the flat stomach, and...

She started, as he turned around and frowned at her. That's when she noticed her phone was ringing in her hand. She quickly turned her back to him, knowing her face was bright red. She answered the phone with a squawk. Cara was on the other end of the line.

"Where are you?"

"We're stuck at some dive of a B&B. Listen, I need to give you the details before the line cuts out. If we don't come home tomorrow, call 9-1-1, because this place is like from a horror movie."

She ignored Hayden's deep laugh. She breathed a sigh of relief as he went into the washroom, closing the door behind him. "Is Cassy okay?"

"Of course she is. We're just hanging out at home."

The line went dead. Ugh. She stared at her phone and grimaced as the bars on the screen went blank. She heard the sound of water running and unbuttoned her coat, placing it on top of Hayden's. She would have opened a closet door, but she'd never been a fan of creepy, dark closets. She was actually surprised how well she was handling this situation. It could have something to do with the fact that she wasn't up here by herself.

Hayden came out of the washroom. "You're going to want to avoid the shower. I pulled the curtain shut. I'd suggest not opening it."

She placed her head in her hands.

Chapter Seven

Hayden waited until Alex finished straightening the quilt on the bed before placing her bags on top. His attraction to Alex had tripled in the last hour they had spent in this godforsaken dive. Sure, he'd been attracted to her from the first night he met her, but now he was more than attracted. He was very, very interested in her. She had demonstrated a few cracks in the massive wall she'd constructed around herself.

Of course, the attraction part hadn't diminished, because he found himself checking her out and appreciating everything he saw…constantly. He knew she had to be somewhat self-conscious because he'd caught her making jokes about her weight a few times. And he didn't really know what she was talking about. Sure, she wasn't what he'd describe as skinny. She was what he'd describe as hot.

It shouldn't matter to him, of course, because she was only supposed to be the mother of his supposed kid. So the fact that she had a temptingly curvy body should not matter. Nor should he be thinking how great her ass looked in her dark jeans. Or the breasts that he knew, based on his own God-given talent, would spill out of his hands. Of course, the only reason he was even checking her out was because she seemed completely unaware of her…assets. She was wearing a T-shirt with a V because both of their top layers had been wet from the snow. When she'd removed her boring sweater, he'd be blind not to notice.

"I think I need to ask Igor if he has any alcohol for the guests," he said, forcing himself to look away. He was acting like a sixteen year old.

"I'm not drinking anything that man gives us." Her hands were perched on her hips, and her shirt was spread tight across her breasts. She snapped her fingers and shooed him away from the bags. "You are in luck. Matt was on my shopping list. Matt loves good beer. I went to this micro-brewery today to pick these up." She pulled out a six-pack.

"It's a Christmas miracle," he said, smiling as she laughed. Alex had a laugh that could warm him faster than any alcohol. Her whole face lit up and it had almost a musical note to it. What the hell was wrong with him?

He forced himself to look at the bags again. "What else do you have in there?"

She gave him an adorable, secret type of smile and then proceeded to pull out a parade of gifts. Toys, scarves, books, and then finally a bag of popcorn, tortilla chips, salsa, and a box of chocolates. "So you had me walking through a blizzard with a six-pack of beer and the entire contents of a department store?"

She thrust the bag of popcorn at him along with the

beers. "Those are twist-off, so we're in luck. The problem is where to set up. The floor is sketchy at best."

"The bed. Picnic."

"Right." She gave a nod like she was trying to convince herself it was okay.

He propped up a few pillows and made sure they both had enough to lean against the headboard. Except she didn't sit beside him, she sat across from him. He opened the beers. "Who's the food for?"

She held up the box of chocolates. "These are Cara's favorite. The tortillas and salsa are for Kate, sort of a joke," she said with that cute smile again.

"What's the joke?"

Her green eyes sparkled, and she was still smiling while he sat there smiling back like a teenager on his first date. "Well, the night Kate met Matt she was trying to enter into a food-induced coma and she really wanted nachos. But then I found Matt."

"*You* found Matt?"

She nodded proudly. "I hand-picked him for her."

"What does that mean?" He found his smile…not working.

"I picked him out of the crowd."

He frowned. "Why?"

"*Hello?*"

"Are you calling me on a phone?"

"I mean, *hello*, have you seen Matt?"

He couldn't imagine smiling ever again. "I've seen him lots of times. I wouldn't pick him out of a crowd."

She rolled her eyes. "Anyway, the rest is history. I feel really bad because these beers were for Matt."

"Don't worry about him. Here, desperate times," he said, handing her a bottle. "Who's the popcorn for?"

Her face turned slightly pink. "Me."

He laughed. "What kind?"

"Aged cheddar, organic, hand-popped."

"Beer, chocolate, nachos, and popcorn. It doesn't get any better than this."

"All we need is for this storm to end so we can go back home tomorrow."

"Will Cassy be upset that you're not home tonight?"

She put a piece of chocolate in her mouth and kind of did some swirling sucking motion; he forced himself to look away. Having, *wanting,* the adopted mother of his child was not an option. Things would get messy when the paternity test came back and it was time to discuss custody. Feelings would only complicate things even more—sexual feelings or feeling feelings. Neither were appropriate or welcome. He stretched his legs out, concentrated on the food and beer, and waited for her reply.

"Cassy's really well adjusted. Like, I think she's more well-adjusted than I am," she said with a laugh.

He took a sip of beer, smiling as he thought of Cassy.

"She has this confidence, almost an air about her that I admire, you know?" As she finished her voice trailed off softly and she was looking at him with a strange expression. She took a long drink of beer this time but didn't look back at him.

"She's definitely outgoing," he said. "She has the right personality for her career choice, too."

She tilted her head. "Career choice?"

He stretched his legs out. "You know, as captain. Well,

pirate."

Alex burst out laughing.

"She told me I could help out below deck." He laughed along with her. He imagined this is what parents did, talk about the funny things their kids said and laugh about them. He could get used to it.

"I'm glad she's tough," Alex said, still smiling as she looked down at her beer.

"Me too."

"So, what do you think the ghost situation is around here?"

He choked on his beer. He realized she was serious when she didn't laugh. "Uh, non-existent. You can't tell me you actually believe Igor?"

"Why would he lie?"

"Oh, I'm not saying Igor thinks he's lying. I think Igor actually believes there's an Irish ghost wandering around here. But that's bull. He's slightly insane," he added when she didn't look convinced. The wind continued to rattle the one lone window in the room, and her gaze darted around whenever there was a loud gust of wind. "Another beer?" he asked.

She shook her head and then nodded. He opened it and passed it over to her. "Do you want to trade chocolate for popcorn?"

"Sounds good," she said, then proceeded to lick the chocolate from her fingertips. He shifted on the bed and looked away.

"Tired?" he asked when she yawned.

She quickly shook her head. "Not at all. Actually, I was contemplating staying up the entire night."

He stilled, his beer halfway to his mouth. "What?"

She nodded. "You know, I mean, it's already so late anyway."

He looked at his watch and frowned. "It's eight."

"Yeah, well, I was thinking of staying up and reading one of the new books I bought."

He put his beer down and studied the expression on her face, except then he ended up looking at her mouth. It was a damn fine, deliciously kissable mouth, but on the wrong woman. His gaze went up to her eyes and his stomach sank. She looked upset, or worried. He ran his hands through his hair. "There are no ghosts, you know that, right?"

She waved a hand away and totally looked like she was lying. "Of course. I just really like reading," she said, yawning again.

"I'm not tired yet. Why don't we get to know each other?" There. That was his attempt at being nice. This woman had taken his daughter in and been the perfect mother to her. Sure, she had some hang-ups and apparently believed in ghosts, but he didn't like the idea of her being so afraid she didn't want to sleep.

Her eyes narrowed on him. "Why do you want to get to know me?"

He dropped a handful of popcorn into his mouth and chewed while he watched her. He shook his head. "Why wouldn't I?"

She shrugged, the movement sending a clump of hair over her shoulder. Her hair was never really styled, not that it needed to be; it was thick and shiny. Now that it had gotten wet, he could see it had a wave to it. "Well, after this whole thing is settled, we're going to be on opposite sides."

Guilt stabbed him as she looked at him, vulnerable, beautiful. "We don't have to be enemies. I told you when I first came here, that I'm not here to ruin your life. If I'm Cassy's dad, the last thing I'd want to do to my daughter is rip her apart from her world. And you're her mother. I'd owe you. A hell of a lot. More than I'd ever be able to repay you, because you loved her and gave her an ideal home."

She blinked rapidly, and he could see the tears in her eyes. If she were any other woman, he'd lean across the bed, slip his hands into her hair, and kiss her until she forgot why she was crying. He finished his second beer and reminded himself she wasn't any other woman.

"Thank you," she whispered. Hell no she wasn't any woman. She was just a woman he wanted really badly. She was a woman that made him crave things he hadn't craved in a hell of a long time. She was a woman that you made love to, a woman you built a home with, a woman you had a family with. She was a woman you wanted by your side. Shit. He reached for another beer.

"So what about your family back home?"

"I have a dad. He recently turned eighty. He's in great shape though. Still comes into the office most days."

She smiled. "That's nice. You work together?"

He nodded. "Yup. He built the company from scratch. We build mostly corporate or high-rise residential buildings. I knew I would always work with him. He's a good guy."

"Did he ever get married again?"

He shook his head. "My mother was, uh, very special." He was going to add that she reminded him of her at times but that sounded kind of creepy so he didn't. But they had been the same type of mom. Both caring, loving, involved.

"What about you?"

She picked at the label on her beer, not looking at him. "No family."

"Just you and your sisters?"

She looked up at him with a start. "Oh, uh, no we're not actually related."

He didn't say anything.

"We met in foster care. Connected. Bonded. Moved in together when we were adults. Each of us always wanted to adopt a child in foster care...so that's my family. Kate, Cara, the girls...and now Matt."

"How did you end up in foster care?"

She didn't say anything for a few minutes. She opened her mouth to speak but the lights went out, blanketing the room in darkness. He heard her gasp, the only sound besides the wind still howling. "Omigod," she said.

"Don't worry," he said, "it's not Patrick."

She gave a small laugh that didn't sound like she thought anything was remotely funny. "Sure, but I'm not moving from this bed."

"Fair enough. Let me find that lantern Igor gave us." He rolled off the bed and felt his way over to the dresser.

He heard some rustling on the bed. "Can't you hurry up?"

"Just trying not to impale myself as I rescue us." His hand wrapped around the box of matches. In seconds he managed to light a match and the lantern. Now the room glowed softly. Alex was sitting beside his spot on the bed, covers drawn up. She looked young and a lot less like the fearless, I-can-handle-everything woman he'd met that night at the bakery. She looked beautiful and vulnerable, and good

God, he wanted her. She was staring at him and he read the relief in her eyes. It distracted him momentarily from wanting her because then the memory of her being a kid in the foster care system came through again. He sat down beside her, stretched out over the covers, careful not to disturb her side of the quilt. He would have rather have been the one to keep her warm, but for once his desire to learn more about a woman won over his desire to sleep with her.

"So we should probably turn in."

"I thought you weren't sleeping tonight."

She frowned and finished off her beer. He took the empty and placed it on his nightstand. "Want another?"

She thought about it for a second and then held out her hand. He opened it and passed it to her. She tilted the beer bottle toward his chest. "Don't let me finish this beer."

"Why?"

"You won't like me very much. Apparently I talk non-stop."

He grinned. "All right, I'll finish the rest when you're done."

"Thanks."

She swept her hand in the air toward him.

"So back to what we were talking about."

"Ghosts?"

"How did you end up in foster care? What happened to your family?"

"I never met my dad so he wasn't a factor. I lived with my mother for eight years." He was hanging onto every word and had to rein in his patience when she paused to take a few long gulps.

"What happened to your mother?"

She didn't say anything for a long time, and he thought she wasn't going to answer, while she finished the rest of her beer and then looked at it, wincing. "Oops."

"Sorry, I didn't realize you'd polished it off so quickly."

She smiled. She peeled the label off, scrunched it in a ball and then placed the bottle and the garbage on her nightstand. He thought she was going to roll over and fall asleep. "We lived above a little bakery. The owners were this really sweet elderly couple, and every day they'd give me a treat after school for free. My mother was…let's say negligent at best. I was pretty self-sufficient."

"At eight?"

"I had no choice. When you have an incompetent parent, you learn pretty quickly how to take care of them. And yourself. I would do things to try and make her happy. I'd try and make her happier than the guys she went out with."

He wished he'd asked Igor for whiskey as he tried to ignore the sick feeling in his gut.

"Anyway, one Saturday morning…actually, no, it wasn't one Saturday morning, it was the Saturday before Christmas, she said we should go down to the bakery and have breakfast there. I was ecstatic. I thought maybe she was finally going to be happy and have a fun day with me. Maybe she'd think I was a really cool kid and she would suddenly want to spend all this time with me. I thought maybe she was showing me how much she appreciated the fact that I'd stayed up late the night before while she was out and I'd cleaned the entire kitchen and washed the floors. Maybe this would be the day my mom said 'I love you, Alex.'"

God, he knew this was going to end so fucking badly and he just sat there, waiting for it.

"Do you really want to hear this? I don't know why I'm talking about this with you," she whispered. She looked over at him and his insides felt raw and stripped. He hurt for another human being more than he'd ever hurt for himself.

He reached over and took her hand in his, then lifted it up to his lips. It wasn't enough, but it was what she needed, because she started talking again.

"We sat at the table in the window. I kept on blabbering to her how it was so pretty out. Snow was falling. There were Christmas lights in the window of the store. Shoppers had filled the streets, carrying big bags and boxes. I drank my hot chocolate, and I was so happy. She asked me to go and get her a napkin. Of course I jumped up ready to do whatever she wanted because it was the best day ever. And then I remember walking toward our table and not seeing her there. I knew, deep down. I knew."

"What?" he whispered in a voice he didn't recognize.

"I stood at our table and watched her get into some car. She drove away. She left me there and drove away."

"Jesus, Alex."

She waved him off, dropping his hand. "It was a week before Christmas and she abandoned her eight-year-old daughter. Merry freaking Christmas, kid, right?"

"Alex, I'm sorry." He reached for her, but she bolted off the bed.

"I'm fine. I got over it. It's totally fine," she said, wobbling because she'd polished off too many beers. Her arms were crossed, and she was staring at him defiantly, until her chin wobbled.

"It's not fine. How the hell can that be fine?"

Her chin wobbled some more and her eyes filled with

tears. "I know it's not fine. I know. But that's what I tell my-self because I can't change what happened. I can't go back. I can't ever ask her why she did that to me. How can a per-son do that to another human being? She was my own flesh and blood, and for a long time I couldn't understand. I sat there all day, telling the owners of the store that I knew she was coming back, that she had told me she was running er-rands. All these people came in that day. Families, moms and dads and kids, people who actually wanted their own chil-dren. Happy people. And I sat there wondering what was so wrong and bad about me that my own mother left me in a store?"

Her voice cracked and she backed up another step until she bumped into the dresser. He was going to give her one more minute and then he was going to reach for her and comfort her in any way she'd let him.

"Sometimes I just wanted to know if I would ever see her again. I couldn't understand how a mother could walk away. I did everything...everything to try and please her. Now, looking back I wonder if I had sensed from a young age how tenuous our relationship was. I remember cleaning, making her food, wanting everything to be easy and perfect. I would try and help out at the bakery downstairs and the owner was so sweet she'd let me take home leftovers from the day."

He didn't say anything, just took it all in, piecing to-gether the things she didn't tell him. The Sweet Spot Bak-ery obviously meant so much more to her than a business investment. She was trying to reclaim something real from her past. Her control issues, her need to be perfect, were obviously from her childhood, and her belief that in order to make people stay and love you you had to do things for them, to make their lives easy.

"Did you ever look for her?"

"I waited for my mother to come back, even though I knew she couldn't. I waited for her at Christmas, after school, after every good thing that happened to me, I waited for her. And then I grew up and I stopped waiting. I stopped caring. You can't make people love you enough to stick it out when the going gets tough. There are people who are in it for the long haul and there are people who get off on the first stop. I made a choice to only surround myself with people that would have my back forever. I never looked for her. Never. Ever. I don't want to know. As far as I'm concerned if she could do that to me, she is not a mother. Not my mother."

He nodded, admiring that she wasn't filled with self-pity or defeat. She'd taken charge of her life, had decided what she wanted.

"What's with the fear of attics?"

She crossed her arms. "I don't have a fear of attics."

"Uh, yeah. What was that all about downstairs?"

"A normal fear of a weird man that wants to place me in an attic."

He almost chuckled except he knew she was lying, and this whole damn thing was painful to listen to.

"I lived in an attic for six months."

"What? With your mother?"

"Yes. Before we lived above the bakery. Except she would lock me in there all day while she went to work. Some days it was really dark. Sometimes she didn't come home."

"What do you mean?"

"Sometimes she'd stay at...a guy's house. I'd hear all

sorts of weird sounds. Mice for sure. But night time was the worst. I'd sit up there and cry and imagine all these things like maybe my mother was desperately trying to reach me but got kidnapped by aliens. Of course that wasn't true, because the next day she'd come home and pass out on the couch. That's okay, Hayden," she said when he stood up. "It's really fine. Totally over it. Once I started school we moved to the bakery. This was such a distant memory I can barely remember."

"How did you ever survive that? How did you become the person you are?"

"I've met some good people along the way. Cara and Kate and I met in a group home and we clicked. We promised each other we'd raise this family together, that we'd be real sisters, that we'd have the kind of family we dreamed about. We all knew we'd adopt a child. Cassy is my little girl and more than anything, I want Cassy to grow up feeling loved, wanted, and safe. I want her to have a perfect childhood. I want her to grow up to be a strong, independent, loving woman. I want her to be able to look back on her childhood with happiness. I want her to never doubt her security or doubt that she is loved. I never want her to feel like she's not good enough."

"You've done it," he whispered. "She's going to be a freaking pirate. She feels pretty good enough."

She gave him a small laugh.

"That's all you, Alex. No matter what happens, you gave her that."

She placed her hands over her face and though he knew how proud and defensive she was, he stood and walked over to her. She didn't move an inch when he wrapped his arms around her. He didn't question himself, he didn't know if she'd push him away, but he couldn't simply sit there. Her hands were still covering her face, but she leaned against his chest and he rubbed his hand up and down her back. He felt the shudder that wracked her body. He kissed the top of her head, and he knew a part of him was offering her comfort, but he also knew how much he wanted her. He'd been attracted to her the first night he'd met her, but now he was attracted to her on a different level. It had started slowly, seeing her interact with Cassy, at work, now. She turned out to be so much more than he'd ever expected. She turned out to be more than anyone he'd ever met. She was good, and she was kind, and she was a fighter.

Somehow through it all she'd managed to still stay soft and kind-hearted, and he didn't know how that could even be possible. She should be cold and bitter, and she shouldn't be showing him this vulnerability that gutted him.

The feel of her in his arms reminded him that it wasn't just compassion he felt for her. It was raw, real desire. She removed her arms from her face and he pulled back slightly, enough to look into her eyes. He saw the fear in them and he wanted it gone, replaced with desire. "Alex," he whispered, threading his fingers through her hair and tilting her head back.

"What are you doing?" she whispered. Up close, her eyes were even more beautiful, and her lips were more appealing. He placed his hand on either side of her face, feeling her soft skin under his palms. Her lips parted, and her gaze was alternating between his eyes and his lips.

The woman standing in front of him was made of steel and softness, and it was a combination he didn't really know what to do with. They were on opposite sides, yet the same. This was hell, because he truly…liked Alex. More than liked. He had other feelings but didn't know what to do with those, so he'd try and push them aside. That's what he told himself he'd do, anyway. His mouth apparently had other intentions.

"I'm doing what I wanted to do the night I met you. When you had chocolate on your lips," he said, lowering his head. He kissed her mouth slowly at first, not knowing if she'd bolt or kick him. Alex tasted sweeter than he'd ever imagined. Sweet, and so damn sexy. For a second she did nothing, then he felt her hands climb up his chest and wrap around his neck. She opened her mouth and kissed him back with the same urgency. His hands left her hair and roamed her body, tracing the sides of her torso, the sides of her breasts. She deepened the kiss. She tasted of chocolate and beer and better than anything he'd ever had. She made a sexy little moan as his hands grazed the sides of her breasts. He forgot about where they were, who she was, and why they shouldn't be doing this.

His hands fumbled with her sweater and went under, feeling her soft skin beneath his palms. She was breathing raggedly, and when his hands covered her breasts, she whimpered in his mouth. He backed her up against the wall. His thumb grazed a taut nipple through the lace of her bra. She filled his hands and spilled out like he'd already known she would. His leg went between her thighs and she opened for him.

"What are we doing? We can't do this."

He stilled for a moment, his hands resting on her waist. "Why not?"

"You're going to break my heart," she said, pulling away.

"You're here, and you're about to ruin the life I've built for myself. You want to take my daughter away from me. You'll have sex with me and...you'll take off. And if Cassy's yours, you'll take off with her, leaving me with nothing. *Omigod*, what am I doing?" she said running her hands through her hair. "This," she said, waving her hand between them and then giving him a slight push. "This can never, ever happen again."

"Stop moving," a deep, husky voice growled in her ear. There was a large, warm hand on her hip holding her still, and there was another large hand on her breast. She couldn't see any of this because her hair was covering her face, and she needed to get her bearings. She wriggled against something hard, and he growled again. Ah. Hayden. Her body was curled against his. He was behind her. In bed.

Her eyes snapped open, and she parted a portion of her hair like a stage curtain and peeked out. Sunlight streamed through the one window. And then it all hit her. The beer. Her ridiculously candid tale of her childhood. Hayden and his delicious brand of comfort. The high-school-esque make-out session that she had ended abruptly. Then the two of them falling asleep in each other's arms. Hayden had been so...hot...and then so sweet.

She moaned without even realizing it until he squeezed her hip again. "No sounds like that, either," he growled again.

She frowned. "Are you always this miserable in the morning?"

"Only when I have a hot woman in bed with me who turned me down."

"Sorry about that," she said, patting his hand and slowly disengaging herself from him to sit at the edge of the bed. She made the mistake of turning to look at him and cursed herself for her decision not to sleep with him. Hayden was lying there looking like some hot-man centerfold. He wasn't wearing a shirt and every hard line, every perfect inch of him, was on display like some sexy buffet. His jeans were half unbuttoned and lying low on his lean hips. His hair was all mussed up, his face was scruffy, and right now she felt like the stupidest woman on the planet. She had turned this man down? She looked at his face, and his disgruntled expression almost made her smile, but then it almost made her cry because she was so dumb.

"I think I need to get the hell out of here."

"What? Where are you going?"

He jumped out of bed and marched across the room. She tried to not drool at the sight of him. Muscles rippled when he walked. Rock hard abs clenched as he shrugged into a T-shirt. "I'm going to ask Igor for a shovel, which I'm sure he has lots of, and then dig our car out of the snow. And if I can't do that, I'll get it towed. We need to get out of here." He put his shoes on and then pulled on his coat, not bothering to fix his hair. He stood there looking at her, a tempting mix of sexiness and testosterone. Good God, this man had wanted her? And she'd turned him down? "You need to stop looking at me like that, Alex."

She started. "What? Me? What are you talking about?"

He frowned. "Like you want to eat me."

She choked. "What? No."

"Yes. I'm pissed, and you're in denial. Well, your body is not in denial. Your head is."

"All right, back it up there, buddy," she said, motioning backward with her hands. "I was at least very sensible. Where would we be right now if we'd…slept together?"

He buttoned up his coat with quick, efficient motions. "Probably in bed, having sex for the third time." He shot her a look. Up and down her body. "Or fourth."

Her face felt like a raging ball of fire and too many images and feelings coursed through her. She tried clearing her throat. "Water. I think I need some water," she croaked.

He let out a sigh. "I'll go to the car and come and get you once I figure out a way out of this dump."

"Are you sure? Give me five minutes and I'll come with you and help."

"No thanks. I need to burn off some…energy."

And with that he was gone. Alex's knees felt wobbly, and she sat on the bed with a sigh, then she stretched out on it. She caught a scent of Hayden's cologne and slowly crawled toward his side of the bed and buried her face in his pillow. Oh, she was so done. She closed her eyes and inhaled, stretching out her body like a cat ready for a long nap. When had she ever felt like this? Never. She had never met a man like him. It had taken every ounce of self-preservation in-stincts last night to turn him down. She had never, ever been turned on like that. If it wasn't for the fear that he would ruin her emotionally, she wouldn't have said no. And then when she thought he was mad, and she went to sleep on her own side of the bed in the dark, feeling horribly alone, he'd pulled her into him. She had never felt more safe or more wanted in her entire life.

She closed her eyes, wondering when the last time she'd ever slept past seven o'clock was. She took a deep breath of

Hayden and fell into the most wonderful sleep.

Hayden placed a bottle of water and a cup of coffee on Alex's nightstand without waking her up. He also tried not to weep like a baby. The woman currently sprawled out on the bed in a dead sleep was driving him to the point of insanity. Last night had been the beginning of this other side of himself he didn't even know existed, the sensitive, emotional side. It was a side that he was now, in the light of day, extremely unsure of. Alex had completely disarmed him. She had stripped him of all the layers that he thought made him the man he was and left him questioning everything.

He had feelings for her. Lots of feelings, he thought as he glanced at her. Sexual feelings, obviously. Those he expected. Those he appreciated and welcomed. It was the other crap, the protectiveness that had consumed him when she told him about her mother was something he had never experienced. He didn't know what to do with it. He didn't know what to do with anything about Alex. He liked her, enjoyed being around her, wanted to be around her...and he didn't know what to do about that. If she had been any other woman, in any other circumstance, feelings wouldn't be involved and lust would have been easy to deal with.

You're going to break my heart... You want to take my daughter away from me... What was he supposed to say to that? She had basically confirmed she had feelings for him as well. And she'd stated the obvious—he was here to take her daughter, his daughter away. Well, at least take away the life she had created for the two of them. Her life had been too hard.

How the hell did a parent just leave a kid? How the hell did anyone leave her? He was angry for her, and he wanted to protect her. Last night she'd shot him down and he got it, he got all her reasons. Even if he didn't agree with them, he got them. Even though she'd turned him down, the need to hold her had superseded all other needs. That had led to torture of the finest kind. No matter what happened, he was going to help her. Whether or not Cassy was his, he'd find a way to make her dream come true.

She stretched and he had to turn away. She was beautiful in a way that actually made him hurt. He stuffed a bunch of the gifts they'd left out the night before back into the shopping bags.

"Ah! Did I fall back asleep?"

"Yeah," he said, lining up the bags at the door.

"Do I smell coffee?"

He glanced over at her. She was sitting up, her hair a mop around her face, looking so cute when she shouldn't. She shouldn't be able to appeal to him like this, but she was so freaking real. Everything about her was gorgeous and real.

"I managed to dig us out, spotted a Tim Horton's, and got you a water and coffee."

She made a dive for the coffee. "Thank you," she said, taking a sip and groaning.

He looked away again. "I've got this place packed up so as soon as you're ready to leave, we can get the hell out of this dump."

"And everything that happened last night…"

"Will never happen again, unless you want it to." He added that last bit in because, well, hell, he was a guy and if she so much as crooked his finger at him, she'd have him.

She fiddled with the coffee cup. "Nope. Not. Even. Tempted. We can go back to being amicable enemies."

He smiled and walked toward her. He stopped when she held up her hand.

"Okay, totally lying. Very tempted. Next time I see you, be sure to get rid of all that…" She made a circular motion with her finger, waving it at his face. "That scruff. And buy some white jeans. And comb your hair really neatly. No more finger combing."

He wasn't following. "Why? Am I from the eighties?"

She laughed like it was an inside joke. "Never mind. We need to get moving. Lots to do and I'm supposed to be at work this afternoon."

The bakery. He was going to have to do something about that too. But first, the car. "Hey, I wanted to talk to you about your car. I'm going to help."

"Nope. Thank you. I've got it all under control. All of it."

Whatever. He'd never been one to take no for an answer. He'd deal with it himself.

She grabbed her coat and turned her back to him but spoke. "So, um, I didn't get Cassy's DNA sample out. I will as soon as I go back home today. We should still know by Christmas."

He stared at the back of her head and hated that all of this suddenly felt wrong. If Cassy was his, they'd be working out some kind of custody. If Cassy wasn't his … that was the worst-case scenario, because that would mean he'd lose them both.

Chapter Eight

Hayden stared at his father's nostril and begged him to move the phone. "So are you coming home for the meeting?"

Hayden hunched forward in the desk chair of his hotel room and stared into his father's eyes. He couldn't lie. "I don't feel right about leaving. Things are up in the air here and…." His voice trailed off, and he saw the shock on his father's face. The nostril view may have been better.

"But you always run those meetings. And this? I mean, Hayden, we've never acquired a hotel of this scale. Everyone here has been working hard. You've been looking over the plans. All you have to do is come in and—"

"I can't. What if the paternity test comes back and I'm not here?" He felt guilty as hell. But the truth was that right now he didn't give a shit about the hotel or anything that was happening with Brooks Building Group. Maybe that's what bothered him most. He had lived and breathed that company since he was a kid, going to the office with his father every day. It's all he and his father talked about. Until now. Until Cassy.

He should be flying home to meet with the owners of the hotel. He always ran acquisition meetings. He should fly out there and then come back to Still Harbor. Except he didn't want to leave Cassy…and he didn't want to leave Alex.

His father nodded. Hayden could see the skyline behind him. His father was still at the office. "Well, you do what you have to do, son. I've got your back. We'll miss you."

"Tell Bill I'll call him first thing in the morning, and I'll send him all my notes for the meeting. You'll be able to handle it without me."

Hayden could tell his smile was forced. "No problem. You let me know as soon as you hear something."

"Take care of yourself," he said before ending the call.

He stood and stretched, thinking he should head down to the gym and burn off some of this energy he didn't know what to do with. He felt like he was letting his father down. He'd done that once before. What the hell was wrong with him?

His night with Alex had left him wanting…her. And he knew it was dangerous, he knew it was crazy, but he wanted her.

If Cassy wasn't his, he could walk out of Still Harbor and reclaim his old life. That was the hope a month ago, that he had no claim here, that he was a free man. Except he wasn't craving freedom from them anymore. He was thinking about Alex and her loan, he was thinking about Christmas, about what it would feel like to know that he was a father. He was wondering, hoping, that maybe if Cassy was his, his guilt from the past would finally be gone.

He hated hoping and wishing. That was for losers who didn't take ownership over their lives.

Alex smashed Rudolph's face in disgust. Tuttle had turned her down. Again.

She frowned at the pile of crumbs on the stainless steel counter in the kitchen of The Sweet Spot Bakery. At this rate, she'd be here all night. This was supposed to be easy. Tiring, but easy. Seriously, she could probably decorate the Rudolph, Abominable Snowman, and Santa cookies blind-folded any other day. Except tonight her mind was on the man who posed the biggest threat to her life and on the bakery that would soon be taken away from her, which threatened the future security she'd been banking on. Of course, her thoughts didn't just stay there; they inevitably went back to her night with Hayden... Everything was so much more complicated now.

Amicable enemies, that's how she'd described the two of them. So clever. So, so wrong.

She didn't want Hayden to know about the bakery. She was humiliated. She must look like a flake who certainly wasn't cut out to be a mother. The things he could provide Cassy with would blow her away. She couldn't compete with that. She wouldn't be able to compete in a court case with him. He'd be able to afford to keep this tied up in the court system for years.

Except a part of her thought that he wouldn't do that. Maybe. Because of the night they'd spent together. And after. And the entire week after. He'd been at their house every day. He'd spent time with Cassy. He'd eaten dinner with them. All the girls loved him, including Kate and Cara. She had tried to avoid being alone with him. It hadn't been too difficult since she'd had to work so much this week. She didn't want to be alone with him. She was not going to let her feelings for him get in the way of achieving her goals.

"Hey. You should make sure that front door is locked once the closed sign is up."

Alex let out a small yelp and turned to see Hayden leaning against the doorjamb, looking way too sexy and way too self-assured for her liking.

"Omigod, you can't sneak up on a person like that!"

"Exactly. You have to lock that door. Anyone could have snuck in here."

She frowned at him. "Mrs. Cooper keeps forgetting to lock the door." She went back to cutting shapes in the cookie dough, disgruntled by his unexpected arrival, and his gorgeous appearance; she was getting tired of his ability to look good no matter what hour of the day or night it was. He had also not taken her advice to shave, because here he was again, sporting perfect stubble on a perfect face. Bah humbug.

"Well, you should double-check after she leaves."

She pressed the snowman cookie shape into the dough and didn't look up. "Is there a reason you're here? Cassy's at home. Also, no paternity test results." She didn't add that the reason they hadn't arrived was because she hadn't mailed them until the day after they'd arrived home from their overnight stay at The Slum B&B. Then the weekend happened. But she knew their arrival was imminent.

She repeated the movement along the dough, ignoring the sound of his approaching footsteps. "I came to see you, not Cassy. And I know you'll contact me the minute the results are in."

She didn't look over at him, even though he was leaning against the counter beside her.

"I missed you."

She pressed another shape into the dough and pretended she didn't hear him. What did that mean even? *I missed you.* They had seen each other every day when he was busy charming the pants…or whatever…off the entire household this week. He was sweet and funny and kind, and she realized her daughter was right: he was perfect.

"I said I missed you." He pried the snowman cookie cutter from her hands, and she was forced to look up at him. She gave him a serene, bland smile, except the second her eyes locked with his, her heart started hammering. Then there was the feel of his warm, large hand on her wrist. Added to that was his delicious Hayden scent. So many layers, much more than any parfait she'd ever put together.

"I don't know what I'm supposed to say to that. I've seen you every day this week."

He took a step into her. "I miss being *alone* with you. I miss hearing your voice, the way it sounds when it's just the two of us."

Her jaw almost dropped, but she managed to keep it shut. "It sounds normal, like a normal voice, whether it's a voice for a hundred or a voice for one."

"You're wrong," he said, reaching out to gently brush her cheekbone with his thumb. Good grief, what was he doing? "First, it's all screechy when you're busy pretending you don't want to see me. Then, your voice gets all soft when it's just the two of us, and you're not busy being pissed at me." He ended that with a slight smile, slight enough that if she hadn't been transfixed and staring at him close-up, she might have missed it.

"You're here to take away my daughter, remember? I'm not interested in being your BFF."

"BFF? I guess I'll have to make myself clear." He grabbed her wrist and tugged her into him.

"Not a good move, Brooks. I don't like being pulled around like a rag doll."

He gave a grunting laugh that somehow managed to sound sexy. She deserved a medal for self-control, because she placed her hands on his chest. And just as she remembered, it was hard under her fingertips, the beating of his heart steady and strong. "Don't even think about it."

"But I do. I think about it. Every day. Every night. I think about you and want you more. And I don't know what the hell we're going to do about it, but I know you want it too, Alex."

She grabbed a fistful of his shirt, holding on because her knees felt like mush. She was going to cave. She was going to cave and choose instant gratification instead of long-term self-preservation. "You're going to break my heart," Alex whispered.

"I won't," he said. His voice was thick and deep and filled with such raw desire that she almost forgot she was supposed to be pulling back from him. Hayden kissed her like no man had ever kissed her. Yeah, the man was talented with his tongue but it was beyond that. It went beyond moves. He kissed her with a rawness that was real. Every rock hard inch of him told her how much he wanted her, but it was the way he held her, the way he kissed her that told her it went so much beyond lust. And that's what made her forget her fear, her phobia of letting people in and them leaving her.

"We can't do this here," she whispered raggedly.

"Why not?"

"I think it might be a health violation of some sort."

"Then spend the night with me at the inn," he whispered in her ear. His hands were now roaming up her shirt, and she tried to catch them.

"I have like two hundred cookies left to bake. I can't leave."

He groaned against her mouth, a sound that scraped against all her nerve-endings as deliciously as his stubble against her cheek. "I'll stay. I'll bake."

She pulled back slightly. He wasn't joking.

"I can't do this. All my reasons still stand." She stepped out of his arms and hated that she was turning down the only man she'd ever wanted like this. She also hated her reasons for turning him down.

"Then spend the night with me. No strings. Get to know me."

She rolled out a sheet of cookie dough, taking her frustrations out on it. It was like she was running in circles. One minute she could turn him down, the next she was kissing him and contemplating spending the night with him. "This is going to end badly."

"No woman in the history of Hayden has ever said that after spending the night with me."

She shot him a look. "Uh, disgusting."

"Okay, how about this? I don't care if we sleep together or not. I want to spend the night with you, alone. I want to hear your voice. I want to hear your laugh. I want to hold you and not have to think about what will happen when the paternity test comes in. I just want you, Alex, however much you're willing to give me."

She stared into his intense blue eyes and tried to find her voice, but her voice was gone, her knees were weak, and she was caving. If Hayden Brooks was Cassy's father, she'd want him to be exactly the way he was now, because he was perfect.

Alex tossed her keys on the end table in his suite at the Harbor House Inn and then snatched them back up again and placed them in her purse. He stood there and watched her. His heart did that unfamiliar squeezing that occurred when she told him things or looked vulnerable. If he didn't think the sensation had to do with her, he'd probably get his heart checked. She then zipped up her purse and placed it on the ground, beside the striped armchair.

"I'm still not sure about this," she said, turning to him. "I really, really wish you'd turned out to be an asshole."

He laughed and walked over to the desk, pulling out a room service menu. "Let's get dinner. Wine too."

She gave him that look again, the one that told him he was impressing her, but she didn't want to be impressed. "Hayden…"

"What do you feel like eating?"

She looked out the window instead of at the menu he

was holding. "You pick."

He glanced down at the menu, then picked up the phone on the desk and ordered. "Okay. Done. Wine, cheese, steak and salad. Apparently they're hosting a wedding tonight so room service will be delayed. At least an hour."

She was still looking out the window, and he had no idea what to do with this mood. He walked over to stand behind her and caught her stare in the reflection.

"I'm not trying to be nasty or ungrateful."

"You could never be nasty. And I don't want your gratitude. I only want to spend the night with you, however you want to spend it. I'm here. Our lives have collided. I came to Still Harbor to see if I had a daughter. I didn't expect to find you, but now that I have, I don't want to let you go."

She squeezed her eyes shut for a moment. "We can't happen."

He took another step into her and placed his arms around her. She stiffened for a moment but didn't pull away. "I grew up working alongside my dad. I saw the decisions he made with his business. Eighty percent of the business deals he made were based on following his gut. I'm the same. I know a good thing when I see it. I've been alone for a long time. I've been with my share of women. I thought I knew what I wanted in my life. Nothing has ever felt as right as you and Cassy." He felt the exact moment she relented; she leaned into him and sighed. He kissed the top of her head.

"You know this is going to complicate everything, right?" she whispered, shivering when he kissed her earlobe, then the soft skin underneath. She turned to look at him, through him, in that way that he'd noticed from the first night he met her. She had this quiet way of looking at him that made him think she knew a hell of a lot more about him than anyone.

"Alex," he whispered, raising his hands to cup the sides of her face. Her skin was soft and smooth beneath his hands. He slowly lowered his head, his mouth brushing hers as he spoke. "I want you. I want you, and I want Cassy to be my little girl." He knew it was dangerous voicing his real feelings, but there was something about her that demanded truth. He stepped closer to her, smiling as she tilted her head back, her mouth parting slightly.

He reached out to sink his fingers in her hair, pull her close, and kiss her.

She ran her hands up his chest and pulled him in closer. Her soft, curvy body pressed against him, and he felt like it wasn't nearly enough. He lifted her up, walking over to the bed, and sat her down on the edge, not letting go, not sure how he'd ever let her go. He stood between her legs and her thighs wrapped around him, her breasts plastered against his chest, and all he wanted was more. He slid one hand up her sweater. She moaned so damn sweetly as he cupped a full breast in his hand, while the other hand was still buried in her hair.

She closed her eyes and he lowered his head, kissing the corners of her eyes, her ear lobe. He felt her move into him, her hands fisting the sides of his shirt. He kissed her lips, knowing how soft they'd be. She opened her mouth and then things moved fast. Every ounce of self-preservation was gone.

"I don't do this, Hayden," she whispered while fumbling with his buttons.

"Neither do I," he said, pulling off her sweater.

"See, I think you do. Hence the whole paternity issue,"

she said with a smile that looked as though it was supposed to be teasing, but instead looked so insecure.

He forced himself to keep his hands still and not on the half-naked, most gorgeous body he'd ever seen in front of him. "Let's get something straight. You are not a one-night-stand. You are different from anyone I've ever known. I will be here tomorrow…" He leaned down and kissed her because he couldn't finish that sentence. He couldn't make a promise like that.

"You're so beautiful," he said, tracing the lines of the lace bra she wore, the breasts that swelled deliciously.

"Hayden?" She held his hands on her waist.

It almost killed him, but he looked into her eyes and forced himself to stand still and listen.

"Don't break my heart. Don't make me regret letting you in. Don't make me regret trusting you."

He answered her the best way he knew how. He bent his head and kissed her until they both forgot all the reasons they wouldn't work.

"So for the record, are you saying I should have told you that you were my first before or after?"

He gave her a disgruntled look and ran his hands down his face. "Before. Definitely before."

She patted his shoulder. "It's okay. You were okay."

He grinned. Clearly the shock had worn off and arrogance had returned. "I know that already."

"You should have known anyway. Who would I have slept with? Who has the time for that?" She shot him a look.

"Besides you, who takes month-long vacations?"

He cut her off by rolling on top of her and laughing. "Always ready with a smart-ass remark, aren't you?"

"I do like to be quick," she said between kissing him back. "You were definitely, um, amazing, Hayden."

He stopped kissing her and braced himself on his forearms, on either side of her. "You're never going to get rid of me, you know that? This wasn't sex, Alex."

She was contemplating asking him what it was, but the knock at the door interrupted the moment.

"Room service," he said, disengaging himself from her. She watched him cross the room, clearly comfortable in his own skin. She drew up the covers and admired the ripple of muscles as he walked. He slipped on a pair of jeans and then opened the door. He stopped the server from entering the room, tipped him, and took the tray. He shut the door and walked over to place the tray on the table in front of the window.

"I'm starving. You?"

She nodded. "But I'm not walking around here nude."

He gave her a long look and then walked into the washroom. He came out a moment later with a plush white robe and handed it to her.

"Thanks," she said, pulling it on. He leaned down and gave her a long kiss.

Once they were settled at the table, they ate and talked about general things. "You told me about your dad, how about your mom?"

He finished chewing and then put his fork and knife down. "She was great, the perfect mother. She was everything for me and my dad."

Her heart squeezed as his hard face grew tender, the sheen in his blue eyes visible as he spoke about his mother.

"It took us a long time to get over her. We didn't know what to do or how to act without her, so my father poured himself into work and took me along with him. We were okay if we were together. We never really talked about her or about anything personal, but we both knew how important we were to each other."

She reached across the table and took his hand in hers. "He sounds like he loves you very much. Your mother sounded wonderful."

He ducked his head and cleared his throat a few times. "There's something you need to know about me, something I've never told anyone. I screwed up badly in high school."

"Who didn't? I mean, I can't think of anyone who says their high school years were the best."

He ran his hand over his jaw, not smiling. "No, this goes beyond. I was dating this girl Chloe for a few months. We had sex. We were each other's first. She was on the pill. At first we always used a condom. Then, sometimes we didn't bother… Anyway a few months later she breaks up with me. I was surprised but not devastated or anything. I had my own crap going on, and I wasn't in love with her. So the next year we were at a graduation party, both of us toasted, and we hooked up. Afterward, she tells me that I got her pregnant."

He stopped speaking abruptly. His jaw was hard. The only thing moving was his Adam's apple. Repeatedly. She didn't move; she just waited. He finally rested his forearms on his knees and hung his head. "She had an abortion," he whispered in a voice that was so low, so raw that an ache burned through her stomach. He squeezed his eyes shut, and she caught the tremble in his chin. "It was my baby too, Alex. I get she had the right. I get it. But it was my baby. And I kept thinking how I would have raised that kid, even if she didn't want it. If she had only given me the chance. My mom told me when she was dying that she'd be there, one day, watching down, watching her grandchildren. Jesus Christ, I was so fucking ashamed. She would have been so disappointed." He dug his palms into his eyes, and she crawled in front of him, pushing his hands away gently, seeing the tears on his face.

"No, she's not disappointed. She knows what's here." She placed her hand over his heart. "She knows how much you mourned your baby. She knows what you would have wanted. She knows the kind of man her son is. A mother always knows her child's heart," she whispered. She gently wiped his tears, feeling the scrape of his beard, the hard lines of his face, and leaned forward to kiss his cheekbones, his jawline, and finally his lips. She didn't know if he'd push her away, and for a second he didn't respond. But then he groaned and his hands plunged into her hair. He kissed her with a ferocity and need that robbed her of thought. His hands went under her robe, finding her flesh, groaning as he touched her. His expression was dark, hungry, and at the same time vulnerable. She pulled his shirt off and wet her lips at the sight of him.

"You have this power, Alex," he whispered hoarsely against her neck. "You have this power to take me away from everything, to make me feel the moment, to make me believe everything you say." Those were the last words he spoke before he kissed her. He kissed away every single thought she had, every single reason she shouldn't be doing this. He kissed her like she was the best thing he'd ever tasted. His hands framed her face, his tongue taking and giving, and yet still not enough.

Chapter Nine

Alex couldn't believe it was already Christmas. The paternity tests hadn't arrived, so she was taking that as a sign that she should relax and enjoy the day. She was going to let herself be happy. She was going to let herself enjoy this time with Hayden.

Alex's gaze wandered the room, her heart filled and aching with the gratitude she felt. The girls were all huddled on the carpet in front of the Christmas tree. Hayden and Matt were on the sofa talking. Matt's mother and sister were bustling around, helping clean up the mess from the presents. Her gaze stopped on Cara and her heart sank. Cara was standing at the window, and Alex could see from her profile that her thoughts were miles away. She was fingering the tiny locket on her necklace, and Alex knew exactly who she was thinking of. Her eyes filled with tears, and she wished more than anything that Cara would find the same happiness she and Kate had.

"Something's up with her," she whispered to Kate.

Kate nodded. "I was thinking the same thing."

She and Kate walked across the room and joined Cara at the window. Cara dropped the necklace and tucked it into her sweater. She put on her "everything's fine" face and turned to them.

"You okay?" Kate asked.

Cara nodded. "Of course. This was the best holiday season the three of us have ever had, don't you think?"

She felt guilty nodding. "Cara…"

"I'm not thinking about him. I'm not."

Kate reached out to touch Cara's arm. "Okay. It's okay if you are, you know?"

"I was thinking about this little boy in my class. He just transferred here."

She and Kate exchanged a look. Right. She was thinking about her student on Christmas break. While toying with the necklace? "I'm serious, I am," she said when they didn't say anything. "It's weird. He reminds me of Jack, and I don't know why…even the way he looks. And they have the same last name. And I know it sounds crazy. I know it's a popular last name, but…"

Ugh. Omigod, she felt like crying for her. It would be impossible, what Cara was imagining. Cara had confided in them about the boy she had fallen in love with. They had both been teens on the street and even though they'd been so young they'd vowed to get married. But Jack had…disappeared. What her sister was imagining now was heartbreaking. She was torturing herself. "Cara," she whispered.

Cara stepped back from them. "I know it's not his kid, okay? I'm not crazy. What would be the odds that Jack was still alive? That he had a kid, and he was in my class. That's insane."

"Okay," Kate whispered. "We're just looking out for you."

Cara nodded. "I know. I'm uh, going to clear the dishes," she said and walked past them.

"It can't be him," Kate said once Cara left the room.

She shook her head. "He's been dead for years. There's no way. I feel horrible for her."

"I know, me too."

Christmas day in a house with eight women was mayhem. And he was loving every freaking minute of it.

Judging by the stupid grin on Matt's face, so was he. Gifts from Santa had already been ripped open, and now Alex was brewing a second pot of coffee before they got started on the family gifts. Matt's mother and sister were here, and Hayden was surprised at how easily all these people had come together to form some new extended family. It was loud, it was crazy, and it was the best Christmas he'd had since his mother had been alive. He had called his father this morning to wish him a Merry Christmas, and he'd felt guilty. They had always celebrated the day by going out for brunch together.

He looked over at Janie who was snuggled on Matt's lap, her face smiling sweetly at him. All these people felt like family to him, like he'd known them forever. They all came from different places, but somehow he felt as though he was part of them. His father would have fit in here.

Matt's mother came in a minute later and placed a large carafe of coffee and a plate of croissants on the coffee table. "Girls, watch out, hot coffee, okay? And as soon as Alex comes back, we can open the rest of the gifts."

"And Matt don't scarf down this plate of croissants. Save some for the rest of us, please," Sabrina said, plucking a pastry from the dish. He liked Matt's little sister. She was always ripping into Matt.

"Hayden!" Cassy waved to him. She was sitting in front of the tree with Beth, and the two of them were looking at all the tags on the gifts and dividing them into the right piles for each of them. He admired her efficiency and hoped she'd like the gift he bought.

Alex came back in the room, and he managed to snatch her hand and tug her onto the sofa with him. She laughed, her green eyes sparkling. She was happy. He'd made her happy. She tucked her legs under her and curled into his side. "I want to give you your gift," he whispered, kissing her.

"That's not appropriate," she hissed, elbowing him.

He laughed. "No, I have an appropriate one too."

"Okay, girls," Cara said, sitting beside Cassy and Beth. "Go ahead and open the rest of them."

It was like an avalanche. Squeals and screams and then Cassy ran up to him and flew into his lap. "I love it!" she screamed. "Will you help me build the ship?"

His heart squeezed as her little arms wrapped around his neck. He had picked out a gift for a kid, not just any kid, and she liked it. He'd purchased the pirate ship the day Alex had gone shopping in Toronto. "Of course I will."

"That is the perfect gift," Alex said to him once Cassy had run off to play with Beth and Janie.

He felt like a kid, dying to see Alex's reaction to his gift. He pulled out his gift with the red bow and placed it on her lap.

"This is for you."

She frowned, looking at the key chain with the red bow. "What? I don't—"

"Your new car. Well, SUV." He said it as though he'd just bought her something as innocuous as a cup of coffee. Not the keys to a car.

She shook her head and backed away from him "Nope. No, you didn't."

"I did." He laughed and snatched her into his arms and held her there. She didn't hug him back right away because she didn't know what she was feeling. She didn't understand why. She shook her head against his chest.

"Yes, I bought you a car. I want you to have it."

"If Cassy isn't yours," she whispered.

"If she's not mine, you still mean something to me. You need a break. You're a woman that's too good for me, too good for a lot of people. I'm giving you a car. It's nothing compared to the life you gave a little baby with no family." His voice was gruff, and he squeezed her against him. The crinkling of a paper or envelope sounded loud as she pulled back.

"What is that?" she murmured and shifted to pull out a white envelope. "Omigod," she whispered, staring at it.

"What?"

She turned the envelope to him, and his gut slammed into his chest. It was the results from the paternity test. She looked up at him, her eyes filled with tears and then turned to the room. "Does anyone know why this letter was in the sofa?"

Everyone stopped and stared at both of them. Hell. Cara and Alex gasped. He heard Matt swear, then his mother and sister nudged him. But when he looked over at the girls, he read their guilty expressions very clearly. Cassy stepped forward first.

"The mailman brought it, and I said I'd give it to you. But I was watching the Doc McStuffins Christmas special and I brought it with me in here…and I forgot! I'm sorry, Mommy."

Alex opened her mouth, but she couldn't speak. Her hands were shaking and her face was white.

"It's okay, Cassy. When did it get here?"

Her chin wobbled. "Yesterday."

"Okay, well, no harm done. Why don't Alex and Hayden run on over to the inn and pick up that gift you forgot to bring?" Cara said, pulling Alex to her feet.

"Yes, we'll keep the coffee warm and everything will be fine. It will all be good," Kate said, as she ushered them both to the front entrance.

Alex looked up at him and he wanted to help her. He wanted to erase the fear that had transformed her face, robbed her of her happiness, of her spark. "It's going to be okay," he whispered, hoping like hell he was right.

"I can't believe this has been sitting in our house for the last day," Alex said. She was shaking, and it had nothing to do with the cold. She didn't take off her coat, just stood in the center of Hayden's room at the inn. He was standing beside the bed, his coat still on as well. He looked… impenetrable. He was all hard lines and his features weren't soft anymore. He did not resemble the man she'd come to know…or love this last month.

She walked over to him and took his hand in hers. He squeezed it back, and they stood in silence. They both stood there, staring at the envelope, its contents capable of breaking apart their worlds. This, *they* never were part of the deal. Yet neither of them had acknowledged what "they" were exactly. What would happen if he was Cassy's father? That had been the most devastating thought at first, the idea that Hayden could be Cassy's father and then take her away. But lately, the other thought, that if he wasn't Cassy's father, that he could wipe his hands clean of them and walk out of their lives forever…

He picked up the envelope and held it out. "Do you want to open it?"

She shook her head, reading the fear in his eyes. "You do it."

He didn't do anything for a moment, just held her gaze. He gave a short nod and then flipped the envelope over and flicked open the seal. Her heart felt as though it was going to burst out of her throat as she watched her future, her daughter's future, dependent on the contents in the envelope. His eyes scanned the letter and then stopped.

His face went white and then he squeezed his eyes shut. "She's not mine."

Alex tore the paper from him and looked for the words. She couldn't believe it. She couldn't breathe, couldn't form a word. This is what she'd wanted, right from the day Matt had told her of Hayden's existence. This is what she'd gone to sleep praying for. But now it felt all wrong. Now it meant the man who had captured her daughter's heart, the man who had captured her heart…didn't belong to them. He could walk out of their lives.

"Holy shit, Alex. I thought she was mine. I *felt* she was mine." He squeezed his eyes shut and rammed his fists into them.

She wrapped her arms around him and seconds later she felt him hug her back and hold her close. The ringing of his phone startled them, but he made no attempt to answer it.

"I wanted you to be her dad. Somewhere along the way, I stopped wishing you weren't her father."

His phone rang again, and he pulled out of her arms, frowning when he saw the display. "I have to take this call. It's my father's cardiologist."

Hayden answered the call. "What? When? Is he going to make it? Yeah, I'll be on the next flight out."

He turned to her and everything she had believed, everything she had feared came through. "I'm sorry. I'm sorry to leave like this, Alex. I've got to go home. My father's had a heart attack."

She nodded, finding the voice she hadn't used for so many years. "Go, you have to go. He's your family. We're fine… We're all nothing now. Go be with your family."

Chapter Ten

Hayden sat with his head in his hands, elbows propped on his legs, in his father's hospital room. The curtains were drawn, the sound of his father's deep steady breathing, reassuring. He was here, back in Vancouver, but his mind was still in Still Harbor and the two women he'd left there. Loneliness, the kind he'd only every experienced one other time in his life, sat in his body like rot.

He squeezed his eyes shut, trying to get the image of Alex's gorgeous face out of his mind. *Don't break my heart, Hayden. She's not yours. You're not Cassy's father.*

One month ago that would have been the perfect answer for him. One month ago, he'd been living an empty life. One month ago he didn't know people like Cassy and Alex existed. He didn't know a thing about kids. He didn't know a thing about…anything important.

Alex had expected him to leave. That gutted him the most, that she had fully expected if he wasn't Cassy's father, he'd walk out of there and never look back. She had rambled and made pitiful excuses. If the call hadn't come through about his father, he would have been able to process everything. But he'd been reeling from the paternity test, then the excuses Alex was feeding him, then the phone call about his father. He'd been back for twenty-four miserable hours and all he knew was that this didn't feel like home anymore. He didn't want to be here anymore. Of course, he'd be here for his father, but this wasn't home. His home was with Cassy and Alex, and he needed to get back to them.

His father stirred, opening his eyes, and motioned for water. Hayden stood, and poured him a glass of ice water on his bedside table. He attempted to put it to his father's lips, but his father grunted and took the cup from him, and slowly raised it to his mouth.

Hayden smiled. It was good to see him recovering so well. "How you feeling?"

"Like I just had a heart attack."

"Well, according to the cardiologist, it was mild. Very mild. You're lucky considering your age. They are going to let you go home in a few days."

"Yeah, so if it was so mild, what are you doing here? And why do you look worse than me?"

Hayden stretched his legs out in front of him. "It's been a long month."

His father pushed the button on the bed and moved into a seated position. He was looking more alert by the minute. "Wait. The results? Are you her father?"

He saw the hope in his father's face, and he knew his father hoped for a grandchild, another piece of his mother. Or maybe he just wanted to see him settled. "She's not mine."

His father didn't say anything, and Hayden had to look away from the disappointment on his face. "You don't seem happy about that."

Hayden shrugged. "I'm not. And I'm not sure what to do about that. I'm pissed. I'm…I don't know. I feel like I lost something. I've never been around kids, but this little girl roped me in and I felt this connection to her. I fooled myself thinking that I felt the connection because she must be my biological daughter. She's not. But I still feel it; I still feel connected to her."

His father didn't say anything, and they sat in the room like two chumps.

"I didn't know what to do after your mother died. I didn't know how to be a father anymore, because it seemed as though the person I was before, with her, didn't exist."

Hayden looked away from the pain in his father's eyes. This was the most real conversation they'd ever had. His father never spoke about personal things.

"I made the money. I was always good at making money. But your mother was responsible for everything else, everything that really mattered. I always knew it, I always valued what she brought to my life, but I didn't have a full grasp of it until she was gone. I failed as a parent compared to her. I'm sorry, Hayden." His father's voice cracked. Hayden tried swallowing past the lump in his throat. A part of him had the strange urge to give his father a hug.

He cleared his throat. "You were a good dad."

"No, I wasn't. If I'd been a good father to you, I wouldn't have let you grow up in an office or on a construction site. I wouldn't have let you think that being alone was the best thing."

"I liked working with you. You always made me feel smart."

"You are smart. Smarter than me, because somehow you figured out there's a life out there for you, there's a woman with a good heart waiting for you, and a little girl who needs a father. You love that Alexandra woman, don't you?"

He ran his hand over his jaw as emotion coursed through his body. "Yeah. I do. And I wasn't supposed to. I didn't expect to. She just reeled me in."

His father gave a low laugh. "The best ones do. Sometimes you just know. It was like that with your mother. It didn't take me years to figure out she was the one. It took me a week."

"She hated me at first. And then…I don't know what the hell happened. I couldn't stay away from her. I couldn't keep my hands off her. All I want is to go back, even though there's shitloads of snow and ice. But I've been feeling all these." He shrugged and searched for words he normally didn't include in his vocabulary. "Feelings."

His father gave a low chuckle. "I think that's a good thing. Feelings have never been my strength. What little emotion I had shut down after your mother died. But she had it in spades. I think it has to do with love."

Hayden nodded. "Yeah. It's a bit insane all the business deals we've put together, all the risks we've taken, none of them compare to this, to the idea that I've lost Alex and Cassy."

His father squared his shoulders, and lifted his chin, looking more like the man he admired and remembered. "We Brooks men never lose. You get out there, apologize for being a temporary ass, grovel if you have to, and win them back. Make me a grandfather. Make your mother proud. But most of all, live the life you really want to live. Be fearless. Love them, Hayden."

Holy shit. His father had tears in his eyes, and he felt the moisture in his own eyes. His father crooked his finger, and Hayden walked over to him hesitantly. For the briefest second he felt like a kid again. His father gripped his hand and then blinked so that the tears vanished. "Enough of this sappy crap."

"Yeah, hell. I'll leave tomorrow morning."

His father nodded, resting his head back on the pillow and closed his eyes.

Hayden stared at the smile on his face and settled into the chair beside the bed. He had planning to do.

Hayden ran his hands through his hair and swore as he dialed Matt's number again. Matt had answered the first time with two choice words and hung up. He wasn't about to let that happen. He'd just keep dialing until he pissed him off enough that he'd have to answer.

"What?" Matt finally answered.

"Don't hang up the phone."

"Why not? You're lucky you're not here."

"Relax. I never took off on Alex. I'm coming back."

"Go on. This better be good. You left me here with a bunch of highly pissed off women on Christmas. Do you realize what it's like?"

"Sorry, man. I'm flying in tomorrow. I'm going to fix all of this. I just need your help with a few of the details."

"If you can fix this and make Alex and Cassy happy again, then I'll do whatever you need."

Hayden breathed a sigh of relief and let Matt in on his plan. His father listened from the hospital bed, a slight smile on his pale face.

"What did Mrs. Cooper say again, exactly?" Alex looked over at Matt who'd insisted on driving her to The Sweet Spot Bakery, or what *used* to be the Sweet Spot Bakery. This morning when she'd walked by, all the windows had brown paper on them, blocking the view from the street. Clearly the new owner was getting ready to set up shop and renovate.

"When I ran into her last night, she said she'd found a few of your personal items and that the new owner needed you to pick them up today because they're starting the reno."

Alex frowned as Matt pulled into a vacant spot outside the bakery. She supposed she should be thanking him for taking her here, but she wasn't in the mood to be polite right now. The ache that had been in her chest all week was only increasing as each day went by and New Year's Day loomed on the calendar bleaker than ever. She'd been an idiot. She'd set herself up to feel the sting of rejection and abandonment. She had also hurt her daughter badly in the process. At night it would take her hours to fall asleep, and when she did, she'd have dreams of sitting with her mother at the bakery. Then her mother would leave, but in the dream, her mother would turn into Hayden. She'd wake up crying, and the knowledge that it was all true, all the rejection was true, would crush her. She put on a brave face for Cassy. It was still the holiday season, and they all had each other.

Alex put her hand on the door and took a deep breath. "Is someone there to open the door for me?"

"No, but apparently your key will still work. Uh, good luck."

She shot Matt a look. "I'll walk home. No need to wait for me." She hadn't touched the SUV Hayden had given her. It sat in the driveway like a big, bold reminder of what a moron she was. She was going to have to sell it.

He gave her a nod. "Alex," he said as she opened the door. She turned to look at him. "It's going to be okay. You're going to be okay."

She nodded and hurried out of the car as she felt tears fill her eyes. She would not cry in front of him again. She and her sisters had put that poor man through the ringer this week. She heard him drive off as she slipped her key into the door.

She took a deep breath of the cold, December air and pushed the door open. The lights were off, but she noticed a strange glow. She stood there and took in the surroundings, her heart pounding painfully as the familiar objects registered. All the tables had been pushed aside. The Christmas tree lights were on and a large quilt, the quilt from Igor's was spread on the ground beside it. The lantern from Igor's was on the center of the blanket, with a manila envelope beside it. A six-pack of beer, the exact same one she'd bought that night, was on the blanket, as well as the cheddar popcorn and box of chocolates. She blinked away the tears and tried not to tremble. This couldn't be a cruel joke, could it? But then she heard the familiar sound of Hayden clearing his throat. She turned in the direction of the noise and almost wept at the sight of him. He was standing in the doorway to the kitchen, the most gorgeous sight she'd ever seen. He was in jeans and a navy sweater, and the expression on his face robbed her of speech.

"Alex," he said in a voice that made her toes curl and tears prick her eyes again. She crossed her arms in an attempt to hold herself together because if this wasn't what she thought it was…

"God, I'm so sorry I walked out of here that day. I don't want anything else. I don't want any other life than with you and Cassy. I want you. I want Cassy. As my family."

He took the room in two strides, and she was spared the humiliation of weeping in front of him. Instead, she wept all over the front of his sweater.

She felt his lips brush the top of her head and then his hands were in her hair, pulling her head back. The look in his eyes told her everything. It was a look no one had ever given her. The promise in it, like nothing she had ever been able to receive before. It was a promise she gave every day to Cassy. She saw the unconditional love from him. He lowered his head and kissed her, gently at first, and then he demanded, drank, and devoured her mouth until her knees were weak. "Oh God, I missed you so much," he groaned. He helped her out of her coat and his hands were everywhere.

"We can't do this here," she whispered while trying to yank his sweater off him.

He guided her down to the quilt. "Why do you think I covered the windows?"

She laughed against his mouth, as he pulled her on top of him. "That's kind of ingenious."

"I know."

"Did you go see Igor?"

He smiled against her mouth. "Yup. He charged me five hundred bucks for the lantern and the quilt, claiming they were antiques."

She gasped and poked him in the shoulder. "You did not spend that."

He laughed. "It was all part of the ambiance."

"And the popcorn and beer and chocolate?"

"Had my friend Ethan in Toronto pick them up for me."

"I kind of feel like we should talk first…as much as I'm liking your idea of a reunion."

He pulled back slightly, kissed her, and then smiled. He rolled her off him gently and sat up. She stared at him, not really believing this was happening. "I was wrong for walking out of here that day like that. I was shocked about Cassy. I thought you were happy. You wouldn't have to worry about me competing for custody of her. I needed to get to my father who'd had a heart attack."

She reached out to touch his hand. "Is he okay?"

Hayden nodded, squeezing her hand gently. "He's going to be fine. Enough so that he's even thinking about moving here."

She frowned. "What?"

Hayden nodded, a slight smile tugging at his mouth. "Because I'm moving here."

She didn't say anything, because she needed to hear all of it. She needed to believe all of it. He didn't say anything, but he reached for the envelope and handed it to her. "Open it," he said.

She gave him a look and pulled out a stack of papers.

Legal documents. "Hayden," she whispered, her eyes scanning over the words.

"Sweet Spot is yours."

She shut her eyes. This couldn't be happening.

"Say something."

She felt his hand on her knee, and she opened her eyes. "I don't know what to, omigod, I don't know what to say. No one has ever done something like this for me."

"I would do something like this."

He pulled out a small box from his pocket and handed it to her. His eyes were wet, and she could have sworn she saw a faint tremble in his large hand. She shook her head. "What are you doing?"

He opened the box when he sensed she was too floored to open it.

She couldn't breathe as she stared at the large diamond ring inside. It was nothing like she'd ever seen before. She couldn't wrap her mind around any of this.

"This was my mother's ring. My father gave it to her fifty years ago, only two weeks after meeting her."

She shook her head, not looking up at him. "I have this crazy need to either throw myself in your arms or run away, afraid because none of this is really true."

"Oh, it's true. I love you and I love Cassy, and when I was on that plane home, all I could think about was how that paternity test meant shit to me. That's my little girl. She and I get each other in this weird way that doesn't make any sense because we're not related and we've hardly known each other. But she's my kid. And you...God, Alex, I have never loved anyone like I love you. You are everything to me. I want to be the guy that you can count on. I want you to know that when I say I love you, I will love you forever. I will never walk out on you. This ring? This is my symbol to you. It will be a reminder to you when the going gets rough, whatever it is we have in our future, that whenever I walk out that door, I will always be back. Always."

He reached out and kissed away her tears. She took his face in her hands and looked into his eyes needing to see the depth there, the promise, but also needing him to see what he meant to her. "You made dreams I hadn't ever dared dream come true. I believe you. I believe everything you've just promised me. You are the father I would want for Cassy. I know how much she loves you. And I...I love you so much, Hayden. I knew I was falling in love with you that night at Igor's, but it wasn't until you left and I felt this hollowness, this pain that wouldn't go away, that I knew just how much I love you."

He pulled her in and kissed her, just like that first time, except now he kissed her with the depth she craved, with the knowledge of who she was. She kissed him back without fear of tomorrow, without fear of the unknown, without fear of rejection. She kissed him as though she were healed, all her scars faded. She kissed him like the woman she knew she was meant to be.

About the Author

Victoria James always knew she wanted to be a writer and in grade five, she penned her first story, bound it (with staples) and a cardboard cover and did all the illustrations herself. Luckily, this book will never see the light of day again.

In high school she fell in love with historical romance and then contemporary romance. After graduating University with an English Literature degree, Victoria pursued a degree in interior design and then opened her own business. After her first child, Victoria knew it was time to fulfill the dream of writing romantic fiction.

Victoria is a hopeless romantic who is living her dream, penning happily-ever-after's for her characters in between managing kids and the family business. Writing on a laptop in the middle of the country in a rambling old Victorian house would be ideal, but she's quite content living in suburbia with her husband, their two young children, and very bad cat.

Victoria would love to hear from her readers!
Visit her website: www.victoriajames.ca

Bruce County Public Library
1243 MacKenzie Rd.
Port Elgin, Ontario N0H 2C6

CPSIA information can be obtained
at www.ICGtesting.com
Printed in the USA
LVOW11s0159041116
511542LV00001B/21/P